I0546295

BROWNING WITHOUT
A CAUSE

Peter Corris: The Browning series
'Box Office Browning' 1986
'Beverly Hills Browning 1987
Browning Takes Off 1989
Browning in Buckskin 1991
Browning PI 1992
Browning Battles On 1993
Browning Sahib 1994
Browning Without a Cause 1995

BROWNING WITHOUT A CAUSE

Peter Corris

Copyright © 2014, Peter Corris
First published by IMPRINT, 1995

ISBN-13: 9781875892228
ISBN-10: 1875892222

For Bill Garner

For help in the preparation of this book, the writer wishes to thank Jean Bedford, John Baxter, the Marrickville Public Library and Video Ezi, Marrickville.

CHAPTER ONE

When I got back to America after working on *Elephant Walk* with Vivien Leigh, Peter Finch and Dana Andrews involving my being kidnapped by Tamil rebels, charged by a rogue elephant and toasted in a fire-walking ceremony,[1] I made two very rash vows. The first was to 'love, honour and cherish, forsaking all others etc.' Louise Townshend whom I married in front of Judge B. Perfect Walker at the Encino courthouse in the San Fernando Valley. It was Louise's first marriage and my third or fourth, depending on how you count.[2] She looked suitably beautiful and virginal in white (all Hollywood brides manage to look like virgins even if it's their tenth time at bat and they've still got their diaphragm in from the night before), and I looked grizzled, humble and mature — well, I was an actor after all.

My second vow was never to work again on a film in a foreign country. I definitely meant to abide by both of these undertakings and, by my standards, I made a fair fist of the first one. I broke the second within a year by signing up for a part in *Giant*. I can hear you saying that *Giant* was shot in Texas with American actors. True, but if you think Texas in 1954 wasn't a foreign country and that Rock Hudson, Elizabeth Taylor and James Dean weren't alien beings, guess again.

I got back to LA in the early summer of 1953, after Louise and I had taken a long, pre-honeymoon trip around the States finding out if we could get along in the bathroom as well as the bedroom.

Things were looking pretty good. I had money honestly earned in my pocket for one thing, and although I wasn't going to get an acting credit for *Elephant Walk*, I felt sure that the good work I'd done behind the scenes would boost my stocks. It isn't everyone who's faced down a charging elephant with a pistol. Dana Andrews had seen the whole show and was bound to have told all his drinking pals about it. For another, I had the money to pay back Johnny Stompanato and I did it, as they say in the business, toot sweet. I had owed him a lot of money as a result of a long losing streak on the horses, at cards and picking fighters with glass jaws. If Johnny the Stomp couldn't collect from your pocket he liked to keep his hand in at the strong-arm stuff by collecting in the form of cracking your skull and breaking your bones. It was to avoid this that I'd left for England in 1953. A few years on and Lana Turner's daughter Cheryl Crane was to cancel everyone's debts to Johnny with a carving knife. Johnny's funeral was well and cheerfully attended. But that's looking ahead to a happier time.

The first thing I did on getting back to Hollywood was marry Louise, the second was call on my agent N. Robert Silkstein. I did things in that order because Bobby Silk would have had a hundred and one reasons why I shouldn't get married. The only marriages agents approved of were ones they arranged themselves or could see a buck in. There was nothing for Bobby in my getting hitched to an Australian nurse who thought movies were for going to see rather than working in. On the other hand, like a lot of his kind, he was a sentimentalist who approved of the institution of marriage — as witness his own five or six ventures — and would accept mine as an accomplished fact if he had to.

'Dick, I couldn't be happier for you,' Bobby said after offering me a cigar which I declined. Louise's only fault in my eyes were an excessive interest in illness and disease. She was a bit ahead of her time in stressing the connection between smoking and lung cancer and she'd compelled me to try to quit. I felt a thousand regrets as I watched Bobby light up his massive stogie. I knew his prostate was shot so there was always a chance he'd have to slip away for a piss and I might get to have a few draws. This is the sort of miserable thinking tobacco addiction can lead to.

'Thanks, Bobby. She's a great girl. She'll keep me on the straight and narrow for sure. She's already got me to cut down on cigarettes and off hard liquor. I'm fitter than I've been for years.'

Through a cloud of expensive blue smoke, Bobby looked me over like a chef selecting beef. 'Yeah, you look good. I could lose a few pounds myself.'

Bobby was short, not much above five feet, and the slim youth he'd once been was now a memory, preserved only in twenty-year-old photographs. He'd grown two extra chins and looked as if he wore a Mae West under his shirt. He had stumpy arms and I wondered if he could get close enough to his desk to do any writing on it. But then, Bobby didn't do much writing. His method of communication, his weapon and wand, was the telephone and it was unusual in my experience to see him without one in his hand for this long. It must have been almost ten minutes. As if the thought had produced the effect, the phone rang and he snatched it up.

'Silkstein, yeah. Hey, Clark, good to hear from you.'

He covered the mouthpiece and winked at me. 'Gable,' he said. 'He's thinking of coming over to me."

'I didn't think it was Clark Kent.'

Bobby scowled, not liking jokes that deflated his importance. 'Yeah, baby. Yeah, well...Ok. Sure.'

He hung up and puffed on his cigar. 'No dice. So what? The guy's washed up anyway. Ok, Dick. So here you are, and here I am and what do you wanna do?'

'Do? I want to work of course. I'm a bit out of touch. What's coming up?'

He puffed more smoke and didn't answer. I knew that a new style of acting was coming in — one where the actor said as little as possible and when he did speak he mumbled so no one could hear him. Fine for Brando, but I hadn't expected it to be picked up by agents. I stared at him and wished I had a cigarette, or a scotch, or both, and it was only ten o'clock in the morning.

'Dick, Dick, I know you been away, boy. But not on the moon. Things have changed in this town.'

Sure,' I said. 'Got to expect that. Look, Bobby, I'm no chicken and I haven't exactly had a string of hits. I'm not looking for a five-year contract with Paramount. I'm talking a gangster flick with Warners, a Western with MGM...'

He shook his head. 'What I mean. Both dead ducks. All the gangsters shot each other. Cagney and Bogart and Robinson bumped each other off so many times people know what's going to happen the minute they come on the screen. They're yawning into their popcorn. And you know what they're calling Westerns now? Oaters, would you believe it?'

'All right. So what *is* being made? Musicals? War pictures? Horror stuff? Sports? What?'

More head-shaking. 'What's being made is not a lot.' Bobby looked pleased with himself for having said this and I have to admit it had the Goldwyn ring. He whipped a gold pen from his shirt pocket, opened a drawer, took out a notepad and scribbled.

'That's brilliant, Bobby,' I said. 'I'll tell everyone you said it, but it doesn't answer my question.'

He put the pen and pad away and held up two pudgy fingers — both with rings on them. 'Fucking television's kicking the shit outa movie audiences. Takings are down, way down.'

I almost laughed. It sounds strange now with big screens and colour and stereo and video recorders and the mute button, but TV seemed like small beer in the early 50s. It was before *Gunsmoke* and *Peter Gunn* and *Peyton Place* (that is, before good Western, detective or sex shows) and the few times I'd looked at the little black and white screen it was always Ozzie and Harriet or George and Gracie.

Sports were another matter. Rocky Marciano was KO-ing them at the time, and the Rock's fights were always good to watch on TV, especially in a bar with a few like-minded souls. But I couldn't believe sitting at home staring at a piece of furniture would ever take the place of a night out at the movies with all the possibilities that offered. However, here was a man who ate, drank and breathed movies telling me forcibly it was so.

'It's a phase,' I said. 'People want to go out. They...'

'Some phase. I could show you the figures. You've got it wrong. People want to stay in. It's, whatcha call it, sociology.'

I gaped. I didn't know what sociology was then and still don't really, and I'd have bet my last dime Bobby Silk didn't either. But he had my attention.

'Folks are buying their own houses more than ever before. It's where they're spending their dough so it's where they wanna spend their time. It figures. Plus, the houses are getting more comfortable. They got washing machines and refrigerators. Mom wants to look at these gadgets, polish 'em for christ sake. Pop can keep his beer cold. They're staying home. The kids? Well, sure, they're going to drive-ins. Once a week maybe. That don't add up to the whole fucking family going to the movies a couple times a week.'

'I get it. But...'

Bobby waved his cigar. 'Did I say movies got only two strikes against them? There's three, maybe four.'

I'd never got very interested in baseball. I admit it's more interesting than cricket, but all those fat bellies and that tobacco chewing put me off. I also thought it had to be crooked — there were just too many ways to doctor things and it never surprised me to learn that the 1920 World Series was fixed. Still, I was pretty sure there was no such thing as four strikes, but when Bobby was in full flight there was no stopping him.

'We got the House Committee on Un-American Activities bullshit still stinking the joint up. The blacklist. The directors are scared, the writers are scared, some of the actors too. And Warners is the worst hit. All those social issue pictures they used to make, where the system is to blame? That all stinks now.'

'McCarthy's a windbag and a phoney. They're going to see through him sooner or later.'

'They seen through Hoover yet? And he's a *schwartze* and a fag. And there's more. The anti-trust laws took away the theatres from the studios. They can't open a picture big and pump it up themselves anymore. Gotta rely on selling the movie to the publicity machines and if they won't play there's no game.'

'You make it sound like the business is finished. You're looking prosperous still, Bobby. Good looking secretary out there. Redecorated office. What's this style called?'

Silkstein re-did his office every few years. I'd seen it look like a high school gymnasium, an Arab's tent and a French whorehouse. Now it was very plain, with bookshelves and leather sofas and polished wood.

'It's called American. Solid, reliable, homey. And if I'm still poking my nose above water it's because I could sniff the wind. I'm taking on TV people — writers, directors, actors, the works. The future's with TV. Believe me.'

'I can't. Can you imagine watching a movie on a screen that big. How'd *Gone with the Wind* look like that? Ridiculous!'

'You'd be surprised. All the studios are making dough selling their old movies to TV. Last thing. The male stars been dragging the women in for the past twenty years are getting old — Cooper, Wayne, Gable. Flynn's a wreck. That boat of his is a travelling bar plus pharmacy. They all got bags under their eyes and less hair. And this new guy, Brando, is he gonna do it all on his own? Name me one other actor under thirty the broads are interested in.'

I thought about it, and couldn't.

'You see what I mean, Dick. Now you, you don't exactly fit into the fresh face category yourself. Am I right?'

As I say, I was fit and by a quirk of nature I always looked twenty years younger than I really was, but there was no hiding the fact that 'mature' was putting it mildly. I'd looked forward to steady work in character parts, still getting the occasional girl and jumping on the odd horse. Now it looked as if I'd have to think again. I glanced around the room. Bobby had kept the old star photos pretty much in place — Bobby with Bogie (clowning with a gun), Bobby with Groucho (comparing cigars), Bobby with Jane Russell (wearing what had to be his highest pair of built-up shoes), but there were a few new faces I didn't know. I got up and went over to look at them more closely. The men all appeared much the same — blonde types with rugged jaws. I put my finger on one.

'Who's this?'

'George Reeves.'

'Never heard of him. What's he done?'

'Not a matter of what he's done. Nothing much. It's what he's gonna be — Superman. Big series going into production.'

'Jesus, Bobby. Have you no shame?' I moved my finger. 'What about this one?'

'Richard Carlson. He's in a show called *I Led Three Lives*, about a guy who's a member of the Communist Party but really works for the FBI.'

'Terrific. What's his other life?'

Bobby put his cigar down in the black glass ashtray and stared at the Norman Rockwell print on the wall. 'You know somethin', I don't know. I never asked.'

'Maybe the audience won't ask either. This television is for idiots, Bobby. Comic books that move and talk is what it sounds like to me.'

'It's where the money's going to be unless something amazing happens in pictures and I don't see it.'

'Three-d?'

'Don't make me laugh.'

PETER CORRIS

'Cinemascope, then. Don't ask me what it is, but I've heard about it.'

'It just means big. Won't change a thing. So, Dick, I'm glad you're back and I'm glad you've got out from under Johnny Stomp, but...'

'You heard about that?'

'I heard about it. Like I say, there's not a lot around. You reckon this *Elephant Hunt* thing's going to be big? Might help you some.'

I considered the question. The shoot had been a shambles and I'd since been told that Vivien Leigh was having trouble completing her work on the pictures. What with nerves, booze, TB and Laurence Olivier — she had a hell of a lot of problems. Peter Finch wasn't a star yet and Dana Andrews was on the skids. I shook my head. 'It's *Elephant Walk*, and no, I don't think it'll be big.'

He re-lit his cigar, puffed, didn't like the taste and snuffed it out. I was beginning to feel like the stogie. 'Well, then, what can we do? Tell you something, there's a new country club opening up. You could give golf, tennis and riding lessons. I can maybe get you the job.'

I didn't have to think about that. I was too old to give tennis and riding lessons. Golf perhaps, but not all three. And the thought of Bobby Silk taking ten per cent of such sweaty earnings didn't appeal. I shook my head. 'What about some work in TV?'

'I thought you said it was for idiots.'

'What's more idiotic than starving in a land of plenty?'

'I'll see what I can do.'

CHAPTER TWO

So began a period which I'd rather not recall. Only the absolute honesty of these memoirs (and the fact that everyone now is so obsessed with television) compels me to talk about it. For the next year and a bit I worked as a TV character actor and bit player, appearing in shows like *Medic*, *The Life and Legend of Wyatt Earp*, *The Cisco Kid*, *The Lone Ranger*, and, perhaps worst of all, *Joe Palooka*. The TV directors liked my looks — I was big and dark and battered and I could ride and shoot and fall down convincingly. I drank shots of cold tea in plaster-board bar-rooms and ducked and took punches and collected crummy pay cheques until I was almost stupefied by boredom. The trouble was, the work was there and it was steady and nothing else was on offer. I'd rented a nice house in Agoura in the Valley with a swimming pool and tennis court because Louise had so much sexual energy I had to provide something to take the edge off it or she'd have killed me in the bedroom. But it all cost money, as did going to and throwing parties so's not to be forgotten, and driving and maintaining two decent cars. American in those days, of course.

After a while, Louise got bored with sitting around and playing tennis and swimming and screwing and she got herself a part-time job in Alameda Hospital. Louise had really blossomed in California. She was a California girl before anyone thought of such an animal — tall, blonde, suntanned, a real work-all-day and dance-all-night type. She had brains too and I often caught her boning up

PETER CORRIS

on medical textbooks. She was a wow at dinner parties with stories about doctors.

Eventually, everyone who doesn't look like Quasimodo, and even some who do, get swallowed up by the entertainment business in LA. *Medic* was a bit ahead of its time as a 'concept' as the jargon goes. It was hosted by Richard Boone who was to make it big in *Have Gun will Travel* (in which I was shot and killed a couple of times but that's a later story), and it dealt in a realistic way with medical matters. Boone, looking professional and reliable in his white coat, would come on and say, 'My name is Konrad Styner. I'm a doctor of medicine.' Then he'd give the title of the episode and the problem it dealt with. Then, 'Guardian of birth, healer of the sick, comforter of the aged. To the profession of medicine, to the men and women who labour in its cause, this story is dedicated.'

It might sound a little corny now, but it was a hell of a lot better than introductions such as, 'A fiery horse with the speed of light, a cloud of dust and a hearty hi-ho, Silver!' *Medic* was shot in real hospitals around Los Angeles and it was during an episode set in the Alameda casualty department that Boone met my Louise. She was always game for anything and willingly accepted the role of the nurse who battled to save the life of an accident victim given up for dead by everyone else. She looked terrific, did a great job, and was offered a spot on the show, playing the part of a visiting hospital supervisor who popped up from time to time to help get Styner out of a hole. Sometimes she'd put on a black wig and do a bit part, usually when they needed an English voice. Louise spoke with an Australian accent but in Hollywood that equals English. Her work on Boone's show led to other offers and pretty soon she was appearing on TV about as regularly as me.

So there we were, with money coming in, plenty of friends and acquaintances, not in the big time but doing very nicely. The trouble was, we hardly ever saw each other. The television production schedules were murderous — it was usual to be shooting a whole lot of episodes at once and you could be standing around all day just to do a tiny scene, then on again for night work, then riding along a canyon rim as dawn broke. Some of the shows I was in were shot partly in New York and I was spending a fair bit of time on airplanes. Then Louise was taken on as a script consultant for another big medical series. The show never got off the ground but it looked promising for a long time.

'Hi, stranger,' I said one morning when I found her drinking coffee in the kitchen. I'd come in late, crawled into bed and fallen asleep immediately. The birds woke me early and I realised that I had time to sit down and eat breakfast as she was doing herself. I was amazed by this and for a minute couldn't think of anything to say. She looked the picture of wholesomeness with her light tan nicely shown off by her white bathrobe. Everything about her radiated health and vitality. I'd had a few drinks after leaving the set and wasn't feeling quite so chipper.

'Hi yourself.' She buttered a piece of toast and drank some milk. Louise never put on weight and could eat anything. I had to be very careful because I drank about three times as much as she did so I tried to eat one-third as much. Not easy.

'What've you got on today?'

She looked at me as she chewed and swallowed. 'D'you realise, Dick, that all we ever talk about is the business? Mostly griping, too.'

I shrugged. 'That's all anyone talks about in this town. I never heard Douglas Fairbanks talk about anything but two subjects — his movies and himself.'

She poured coffee and added cream and sugar. 'You're just pulling rank on me, showing me how old you are and how long you've been around.'

'I think we're fighting.' I moved the cream and sugar out of reach and poured myself a cup. 'That makes a change.'

She came around the breakfast bar and kissed me. I automatically put my hand inside her robe and felt her full, firm breast. I've got a big right hand, over-developed by tennis, but Louise's breast filled it easily. She leaned against me, hip to hip. For southern California the morning had been cool but suddenly I was warm all over. I leaned down and kissed her as I undid the tie of her robe. A pair of silk pyjamas doesn't constitute much of a barrier and pretty soon we were going at it like steam on top of the table. Probably only an athletic woman like Louise could enjoy the position. She certainly seemed to.

When we'd finished I said, 'We'll have to argue more often.'

'We weren't arguing, we were talking and that's what's unusual.'

I grunted. Like most men, I can never see the point of talking about talking. I was experiencing a warm glow and thinking about a cigarette and a cup of coffee, maybe with a shot of brandy in it to help the glow along. Louise put on another pot of coffee and tossed her cold toast out onto the grass for the squirrels that inhabited our big garden. I lit the cigarette but didn't reach for the brandy. She didn't like to see me drinking in the morning and I was in a mood to oblige her.

'Dick,' she said as she poured me a cup of coffee. 'What do you really want to do with your life?'

They say your whole past flashes before your eyes when you're about to die. That hasn't happened to me and I've been close enough to the finishing line enough times for my evidence to be worth something. In my experience, that phenomenon only occurs when a woman asks a *big* question of the sort Louise put to me then. I'm not sure why this is and I'm not inclined to shell out thousands of dollars on a shrink to get an opinion. At a guess, it's just a mechanism that helps you to avoid an answer. I was re-living a particularly disgraceful episode that took place in Canada[3] when I heard a strange sound. I looked up and saw the coffee cup rattling in the saucer with the force of my shaking hand.

Louise laughed. 'Dick, I can read you like a book. Don't worry, I'm not pregnant and I haven't had a letter from my mum saying she wants to come and visit.'

Somehow I stopped trembling and took refuge behind a smoke screen. 'What's on your mind then?'

'I can see an opportunity. I can smell it and taste it. I'm never wrong in these things. I felt like this when I first heard about the nursing course and then again when the chance came to get out of Australia. I felt it again when I met you.'

'I'm not sure how to take that.'

'Take it as a compliment. When I think how I could be back in Artarmon, married to Dr Talbot. That's when *I* tremble, brother.'

All very comforting that, but I was still wary. A squirrel jumped out of a bush, picked at a piece of toast, grabbed it and shot out of sight. Not a bad strategy. I was tempted by the thought of the brandy again.

'Christ, look at the time,' Louise said suddenly. 'I'm supposed to be on the set in an hour. I've got to rush.'

'Hey, hey. You can't go now. What's all this leading to? I'm hanging on by my fingertips here.'

She dashed past me. 'Tonight, lover. Tonight. We'll eat out, drink some wine and discuss it.'

'It! What the fuck is *it?*'

But she was gone and I felt too drained to follow her upstairs and pursue the matter. A woman showering and dressing for a fast exit has a dozen ways of deflecting questions. *Throw me a towel. Where's my bag? Start my car, please, darling.* Instead, I grabbed the brandy.

I spent the morning in a haze of anxiety and alcohol and only a long session in the swimming pool got me in shape to muddle through the afternoon. I was working in an episode of *The Cisco Kid.* The scene called for me to jump off a horse, knock a man down and call him a son of a dirty dog, in Spanish. Nothing much to it. The

13

hardest bit was not tripping over in the jingling, flared-bottom trousers the costume people always put Mexican bandits in. The pants had silver coins attached to the outside seams. I'd seen a few Mexican bandits in my time, too close up for comfort, and I could have told them that they wore anything they could steal and that any silver a bandit happened on travelled immediately across the bar in the nearest *cantina.*

Languages and horses are two things I've always been good at and the scene was giving me no trouble until the director insisted that I was mis-pronouncing the words. He bleated out some musical stuff that might have sounded good in Madrid or in Spanish III at UCLA, but wouldn't have been understood at all south of the border.

'The guy's a Mexican thug, for Christ sake,' I said. 'He wouldn't talk like a faggot florist.'

Bad mistake. The director was a homosexual and no cream puff. He was one of those homosexuals who feel impelled to prove how tough they are and he took a swing at me, connecting lightly. Ordinarily, I'd have let it go, laughed it off, tried to make some mileage out of it. Directors aren't supposed to punch actors. They can fuck them in a variety of ways but not hit them. But I was out of sorts, worried about what Louise was plotting and feeling a morning booze headache coming on. I swung back and landed solidly on the director's jaw. I heard that awful sound a bone makes when it breaks and felt it in my gloved fist as well. The glove helped the punch along — instinctively, you don't hold back when you've got a glove on. He went down as if someone had cut the legs from under him.

I heard later that they'd kept the cameras rolling and that the film was later played at parties, but at the time there was no fun to be had. Everyone went quiet and still and the director lay on the ground and didn't move. Eventually, one of the female production assistants rushed forward and lifted his head and confirmed that he was still breathing. She ran off to call an ambulance — no mobile phones in those days — and everyone looked down at the man lying there with his jaw pointing towards his left shoulder. I did the only thing I could do — swing myself up onto my horse and ride away. I believe they got that on film too.

Nobody spoke to me. I changed out of my costume, took off my makeup and signed myself off the lot. When I got out to my car I realised that I'd put the riding gloves in my pocket. I've still got them somewhere, a memento of the best punch I ever threw. I drove home in a kind of daze, aware that I'd just put an end to my career in television. They'd put up with drunks and hopheads and nymphomaniacs and people who couldn't get anywhere on time, but not actors who king-hit directors. I wandered around the house picking up various bottles and putting them down. I sat by the pool and thought about taking a swim but didn't have the energy. When the phone rang I knew exactly who it would be.

'You crazy fuck,' Bobby Silk spluttered. 'The fuck you think you're doing?'

'I didn't think. He hit me, I hit him back.'

'You hit him. Ok, accidents happen. But did you apologise? Help the poor bastard into the ambulance? Ride to hospital with him? Talk to...'

'Kiss his ass? No, I didn't, he had it coming.'

'Is that right. Well, I'll tell you what you got coming in the way of work, Dick — nothing!'

We both hung up. By then the sun was touching the tops of the pines and I had a drink. I'd had quite a few drinks by the time Louise got home but I managed to suit up and take her out to dinner at a new fancy roadhouse off Ventura. Louise ordered a big steak, of course, and I pushed something around on a plate while I tried to get up the courage to tell her I was unemployed. Luckily, she was full of her own idea.

'A school,' she said. 'A school where we teach them to ride and swim and dive and play tennis and golf and shoot and all the other things you and I can do really well but they can't do for nuts.'

Her enthusiasm got to me and I laughed. 'What about act? You left that out.'

'Someone else can do that. How many times have I heard you raving about what clumsy, unathletic clods most of them are? You've taught a few actors some tricks in your time anyhow, haven't you?'

'I taught Gary Cooper to shoot for *Sergeant York*,' I said. 'At least I taught him how to *look* as if he could shoot. He never was much good at the real thing.'

'That's what I mean. You'd be a natural. We could charge some whacking great fees. The studios'd pay for some of them. We couldn't miss.'

My last significant business venture had come totally unstuck and left me with sour memories of the whole thing.[4] I took a swig of the California red and prepared to bring her back to reality. Did I say that she was looking terrific in a pale blue linen dress with a white silk jacket? 'It's a great idea, love, but you'd need a hell of a lot of capital to set up something like that. You'd need land and facilities and ...'

'We can get the capital. One phone call and it's all wrapped up.'

I had to tell her then. I drank some more wine and gave her the whole sorry story, including the sentence of professional death passed on me by N. Robert Silkstein. I expected tears or anger. Instead she leapt from her seat, came around the table and gave me a lingering passionate kiss. 'Darling,' she said, 'that's brilliant! That's wonderful! Rebellion's the coming thing. You'll be notorious. They'll be coming to us in droves!'

CHAPTER THREE

SHERMAN House was one of the nicest places I've ever lived in. We had fifteen hilly and lightly-wooded acres on the outskirts of the little valley town of Sherman Oaks, complete with stream, stables, tennis court, pool, practice golf hole and gymnasium. The house was a mock Tudor affair, white stucco with stained timber strips on the exterior and lots of exposed beams inside. It had six bedrooms and plenty of space for entertaining, including a sizeable room with a small dance floor. Both Louise and I were expert ballroom dancers and this was another talent we had on offer. There were four cabins in the grounds where long-term students could stay — at a pretty steep price. The one-year lease cost a bomb but somehow Louise and her mysterious backer took care of that.

Before I could turn round I found myself the employer of two assistant sports coaches, Matt Pendle and Sue Larch, as well as a groundsman, horse-handler and a couple of inside staff. As Louise had expected, a few judiciously placed ads in the trades and a flock of phone calls from the pair of us brought a quick influx of students which turned into a steady stream — most of them lusting for fame in movies or television, some subsidised by the studios who had them under contract, some backed up by rich parents indulging them in their fantasies. There were even a few who worked like slaves at part-time jobs to raise the fees while they fitted in lessons between pumping gas and turning up at auditions. Poor fools, the exhaustion was obvious in every move they made and their clothes and bad skins and neglected teeth showed that they were from hunger.

All in all, it was a pleasant life, especially as I was able to concentrate on the better students — the ones who had *some* hand-eye co-ordination and could control a ball. After a while a few of them were capable of a decent set of tennis and a round of golf where I didn't have to carry a box of balls in my bag. I have to admit that there were some fair swimmers among them and, if there had been any call for more swimming movie stars than Esther Williams, we could've met the demand. But there wasn't. The real duds I assigned to Matt and Sue who didn't like it but were paid to put up with it. Things worked out pretty much as Bobby Silkstein and Louise had anticipated — I got no offers of parts in the established TV shows or the ones that were being planned, but plenty of sulky-looking kids with long hair and dangling cigarettes wanted to learn how to be a horse-riding, rebellious, fuck-you, two-fisted actor.

That led to the first serious argument with Louise. Again, we weren't spending a lot of time together, busy giving lessons and often too tired at night for more than a brief kiss or a quick coupling. For this pitch, I *made* some time, insisting that Louise join me for a quick picnic in a quiet spot near the stream. I even made the sandwiches.

'They want it,' I told her, taking the top off a bottle of beer. 'They *all* want it. They're hungry for it.'

I was referring to the crying need for a boxing instructor. Almost every kid who came our way had heard how I'd decked the director and wanted to learn to box. Some thought they could fight already, were anxious to take me on, and I had difficulty in fending them off.

'No,' Louise said. 'I can't stand boxing. It's ugly and brutal.'

'Have a drink and be reasonable. We'd make money. Boxing pictures never go out of fashion and a lot of actors fancy themselves up there in the ring.'

'I don't want a drink. I have to give a show-jump class this afternoon. No boxing. What about fencing? We could do that instead.'

'Fencing's no substitute for boxing. Nothing is.'

'I agree. So let's forget fighting of all kinds. This is a skills academy and ...'

'A what?'

'An idea of mine. To put on the new brochure. The Sherman Oaks Skills Academy. Lots of class, don't you think?'

I didn't have a lesson to go to so I drank all the beer. I found it hard to stay mad at Louise. She was so nice and decent and good-natured that antagonism just seemed to melt away when she was around. I suspect she'd got her own way all her life because of this power she exerted. She certainly got her own way in all her dealings with me. Still, I harboured a little background resentment. I'd always liked the fight crowd, found them interesting, and I would have enjoyed some sort of connection with them. I'd even had in mind the right guy to hire as a part-time boxing coach — Rocky Graziano.⁵ The Rock was a few years past his world middleweight title days and his all-out wars with Tony Zale, and he was hanging around Hollywood picking up bit parts as a heavy. I'd met him a few times in night clubs and knew he was a fun guy. He'd be glad of the work and I'd enjoy putting on the gloves with him myself, as long as he had it clear that you don't damage the boss.

So I was mildly annoyed and slightly disappointed. I thought Louise had mis-judged. My business sense is nil and it's not often I get a winning idea — when I do, I don't like to see it going to waste. I wouldn't say I neglected my work at the skills academy — I rode and swam and whacked balls as before, but my heart wasn't quite in it.

I was out in the horse paddock one day, trying to catch Old Smoky, one of the stallions, that didn't want to be caught. He was a playful horse rather than mean, and he liked to skitter around, ducking away from the lariat and making the roper look foolish.

There was a slight edge to the game — he wasn't above rearing up and flashing his hoofs at you if you didn't enter into the spirit of the thing. I was racing around the corral, churning up dust and trying to line him up for a good throw when I heard the roar of a motor cycle engine close by. We didn't allow motor cycles on the property because the noise can spook the horses and we were always likely to have some beginner riders around who might get into trouble.

I looked around for the culprit. Old Smoky misinterpreted my action and lashed at me. Quite by instinct I ducked away, took two steps back and threw. The noose took him cleanly and tightened as smoothly as you could wish. Smoky was a sport. He calmed down and stood quietly, panting a little and glaring but not offering any further trouble. I patted him, secured him to a rail and marched off in the direction of the motor cyclist who had dismounted and was leaning against the barred gate with a cigarette hanging from his mouth. I climbed over the gate, twitched the cigarette out and stamped on it.

'Didn't you see the sign? No motor cycles. Or maybe you can't read.'

'Uh, now don't get all riled up, sir. I'm sorry. I didn't see no sign, but I sure did see you rope that horse. You think you could teach me to do that?'

When I'm faced with naked admiration for something I've done I tend to warm to the admirer. There was something familiar about this shortish, slight but strong-looking young man. He had thick brown hair brushed back and tousled from riding the bike. He looked tough and soft at the same time as he fished his cigarettes out of the pocket of his flannel shirt. He picked one out of the soft pack and held it out to me almost as a peace offering.

I shook my head, not willing to give him the edge. 'We give lessons,' I said. 'You can learn, if you pay the fees.'

'Uh, well, I don't know about that.' He looked down at his motorcycle boots as he spoke. 'I was kinda thinkin' you might just give me a pointer or two.'

'Sorry, son. It's strictly business around here.'

'Oh, that's too bad. I thought it might do you some good if it got around I was kinda taking an interest in your place.'

I wanted to give him an uppercut for his arrogance and to get him to lift his head. He was still looking at his boots. He'd lit the cigarette and smoke was drifting up past his face. It's hard to tell from the top of someone's head, but I was sure that I knew him from somewhere.

'Who the hell are you?'

He lifted his head, stuck out his hand and gave me the full candlepower of his actor-hustler smile. 'I'm a new neighbour of yours, Mr Browning. Name's Jimmy Dean.'

CHAPTER FOUR

East of Eden and *Rebel without a Cause* hadn't yet been released and although there was already a lot of publicity about Dean, I hadn't seen him on screen and his photographs didn't look a hell of a lot like him. He was much shorter than you'd expect and I guess younger-looking. I knew the name and the expectations a lot of people had of it, but I wasn't about to fall down and start licking his motorcycle boots.

I shook his hand, feeling the old callouses on it and the strength in his grip. 'Well, Jimmy, I'm glad to meet you. Heard a bit about you, but rules are rules. And the rule around here is — no motorcycles.'

He sucked on his cigarette and let the smoke out slowly in a way I wouldn't have let him do if I'd been his drama coach — way too stagy. 'How'd you suggest I go back down the track then, Mr Browning, sir?'

'I'd suggest you wheel it, until you get out of the hearing of the horses. Wouldn't be more than a hundred yards or so. That sound like a fair thing to you?'

He didn't like it. The cycle was a big Harley hog and he was a little guy, but he could see that the alternative could be something worse — like being knocked on his ass with a few people watching. Still, he gave the old charm one more try. 'Not very neighbourly.'

BROWNING WITHOUT A CAUSE

'I'm running a business,' I said. 'I've got people to look after. But I'd be glad to give you a few roping lessons anytime you're ready. Just drive up or walk. Your choice.'

He let his cigarette drop from his mouth and stamped on it the second it hit the ground — neat trick. Then he threw his head far back and let out a hearty and natural-sounding laugh. If he was acting now he was good, very good. 'Heard you was a hard case and I see you surely are. I just might take you up on that, about the lessons.'

'Do that.'

He twisted the handlebars around and wheeled the bike in a wide arc. Then he pushed it away down the track. The slope was in his favour and he did the pushing easily, which wasn't what I had intended but might have been something he'd noticed. He kicked the starter and had the engine roaring at a point more like sixty than a hundred yards away, but I figured that I'd come out of the confrontation about even.

I told Louise about it later, including how I'd sent Dean away with a flea in his ear. She stared at me.

'Honestly, Dick, you must be losing your marbles. He's the hottest thing in Hollywood, or will be. Everybody's talking about him. Our stocks would go through the roof once word got out he was here. And we could make damn good and sure that word did get out.'

'He's a punk,' I said. 'I've seen them come and go over the years. A flash in the pan, and if you let one of these freeloading beatnik types take up space around here you'll be feeding hordes of them before you can spit.'

'He's hardly a beatnik. He's got a contract with Warners.'

'You know what I mean.'

'I think you let a great opportunity slip.'

I'd had a few drinks by this stage and wasn't prepared to lie down for her. 'And I think you're wrong about the boxing. I think *that's* an opportunity. Tell you what — you give in on the boxing and I'll give in over Dean. I'll even find out where he lives and make an approach to him. What d'you say?'

Louise hated a compromise the way a cat hates water. She hummed and hahed and tried to talk me around on Dean without conceding anything, but I stuck to my guns. 'No boxing, no Dean. And don't think you can charm him into hanging around here. You'd be wasting your time.'

'What d'you mean by that?'

I'd spoken without thinking and had to stop to consider what I *had* meant. On thinking about it, I was pretty sure he batted for the other side, or at least played on both teams. Just something about all those mannerisms — very narcissistic and sexually challenging. I didn't want to get into that with Louise though; 'I backed him down,' I said. 'That got his attention away from himself for a second or two. I'd say he respects me.'

'He's going to be huge.'

I laughed. 'You should see him. He'd come up to about your ear, if that.'

'You know what I mean. We really need someone like him.'

That alarmed me. '*Need*? I thought you told me the place was doing fine.'

'Oh, it is, it is. But, you know, the overheads are high and what with one thing and another... '

I didn't know and I didn't want to. Business has always confused and depressed me, especially when it's going badly and I've never forgotten the advice Machine Gun Jack McGurr[6] gave me in Chicago in the 1920s when the air freight outfit I was a partner in was facing bad times: 'Rob a bank,' Jack had said. From what I've seen of it, that's often the only way to save a business that's on the skids. This time around I'd made a definite decision to leave all the management side of things to Louise and to take as big a salary as I could get my hands on and not worry. The trouble with deciding not to worry is the worry it creates. Still, I tried to apply the philosophy.

'Ok,' I said. 'I'll talk to Dean. But the rule sticks — no motorcycles.'

'Hmm, yes. I've heard he's a speed demon. Warners are worried about him killing himself.'

'Yeah, before *they* can kill him with work. Around here he drives slowly, walks or rides a horse — if I can find one little enough for him.'

'Fine, and as for your boxing cronies, I don't want to see any cauliflower ears or punch-drunk bums. Sherman House is supposed to inspire confidence, not show what happens to people who like to pretend they're back in the stone age.'

'Boxing started in Greek and Roman times actually, I said, remembering a conversation I'd once had with Nat Fleischer.[7] 'Very cultured lot the Greeks and Romans. Lord Byron was a boxer, so was Bernard Shaw and...'

Louise sniffed. 'Shakespeare, I suppose.'

I sniffed, shuffled my feet and threw a few jabs. 'Coulda been.'

We got through it like that, amicably enough, but it ushered in a combative tone to our relationship. When we played tennis or golf together from that time on, Louise tried extra hard to beat me and, with her youth advantage and the handicaps I gave myself, she sometimes did. I was trying hard too. As an example of what I mean, I set about putting *my* idea about the boxing into practice before I did anything about James Dean.

The first thing I did was phone Lou Cohen, an agent who handled people like Rocky, Max and Buddy Baer, 'Slapsie' Maxie Rosenbloom[8] and other ex-fighters, as well as stuntmen and bit players — what you might call the rougher element.

'Hey, Dicky, boy. Great to hear from ya. What can I do in your interest? Just name it.'

Now that was strange. I'd only met Cohen once or twice and although we'd got on all right I didn't think of him as a pal. And he wasn't being ironic. He sounded genuine, which, in Hollywood doesn't mean quite the same thing as any place else. What it means is that for reasons that suited *him* he was willing to give me his full attention and cooperation. Very unusual.

I told him what was on my mind and he was falling over himself to help. He said the Rock wasn't busy, thought the world of me, had heard the best of my establishment and that he could guarantee to deliver him to my door any time I wanted. I was suspicious but what could I do? I was getting what I wanted, a rare state of affairs in Hollywood. We agreed that Rocky should come out to Sherman House the following day.

'Anything else?' Cohen said.

'No, Lou, that's all. Thanks.'

'My pleasure.'

I was sitting in the office where I spent as little time as possible because filing cabinets are not my favourite pieces of furniture. I stared at a framed photograph on the wall, not recognising the smiling, handsome young face. I got an almost physical shock when I realised that the face was mine. Somehow, Louise had dug up a still from one of my old movies and had it cropped and blown up. To judge from the cut of the suit I was wearing it was from twenty years ago at least. I was thinner with no grey in my hair and an optimistic cast to my features. Hard to look like that after all I'd been through in the intervening years. I wondered about Louise's motive and why she hadn't mentioned the picture to me. I began to wonder a lot of things about Louise.

You can buy almost anything in Los Angeles if you know where to look. Small boxing clubs were closing down all over town as TV took away the live audience. I knew that the Butterfield, a club in west LA I'd gone to for years, was folding and selling off all its equipment. I drove down there in the company pickup and bought the ring and everything that went with it for a couple of hundred dollars. I also hired the guy who'd dismantled it to re-assemble it back at Sherman House under an awning behind the stables. I wasn't going to push Louise too hard by setting it up right under her nose.

The job was well-advanced when Rocky Graziano arrived in a two-tone Buick at eleven o'clock the next day. For some reason, fighters never go anywhere alone. The Rock had 'Tank' Tranter with him, a former light-heavy weight who also worked in the movies. Some people thought Tank's nickname described his build which was low and wide, but those in the boxing game knew it referred to the number of fights he had thrown. His relatively unmarked face was another giveaway. Rocky was slightly over-dressed as usual, in a checked sports coat, hand-painted tie, gabardine slacks and wing-tips. Both he and Tank looked nervous as they approached me. I put it down to their upbringing: Rocky was from New York's East Side and Tank had been born and raised in Chicago. They were probably worried by the number of trees and the absence of moving automobiles.

'Hey, Dick,' Rocky said, glancing around him as if he expected Tony Zale to jump out from behind a tree. 'How you doin'?'

'Not bad, Rock. Hi, Tank. Come and have a look at the set-up.'

I escorted them to where the ring was being put together. Both men kept glancing around nervously and I began to wonder if they were on something. Cocaine and benzedrine were big in Hollywood at that time, and every second person you met was twitching like he had an attack of St Vitus dance. The ring was almost ready and I have to admit I was somewhat dismayed by its appearance. The stained canvas and frayed ropes hadn't looked too bad inside under lights in the middle of a thick smoke haze. Out here, with the sunshine falling on part of it, the ring looked almost derelict. You could almost see the ghosts of the old fighters, smell their blood and sweat and hear the howls of the crowd which gave rise to very mixed feelings.

Tank wasn't impressed. 'Geez, Rock, it looks as if it dates back to John L. Sullivan.'

'It's authentic,' I said. 'The kids should know what the business is really like.'

'They're anything like the powder puffs I been meetin' around here,' Rocky said, 'they'll run a friggin' mile.'

Not encouraging. Rocky and Tank both looked as if they'd rather be somewhere, almost anywhere, else. They refused a drink and after he'd agreed to be on call for a few exhibitions and lessons when the ring was ready, Rocky almost sprinted back to his car and roared away. So much for hiring a fan guy who'd put a little life into the place. I was depressed and became short and testy with the guy setting up the ring. I told him to wash the canvas and he looked at me as if I was mad.

'It'll shrink.'

'Then stretch it.'

A few days passed, days spent squabbling with Louise and trying to avoid the most inept of the students. It's impossible to look good playing tennis against someone hopeless or constantly having to dismount to help someone who's fallen off. After a while, your own technique goes off and you end up impatient and frustrated. I discovered at Sherman House that I wasn't made of the stuff true teachers are made of. It was one thing passing on a few shooting tips to 'Coop' or working on Katie Hepburn's backhand,[9] and quite another messing about with un-coordinated duds. I lost my temper a couple of times and yelled at the students. They appealed to Louise and she gave me the edge of her tongue.

'You're a fool, Dick. We've had two students walk out on us today because you shouted at them. They were both signed up for a lot of stuff, too. Do you want to send us broke?'

We were in that little office with Louise sitting behind the desk and me leaning against one of those bloody filing cabinets. It was too small a space to have a fight in. I like to pace when I work up a head of steam and this was cramping my style.

'I couldn't help it. They were useless. You could give them lessons all day and all night for a month and they'd still be hopeless.'

'That isn't the point. We need the money!'

Her seriousness brought me up short. As I've said, I took no interest in the financial side of things, but this wasn't the first time she'd brought up the question of the cash flow. When I thought about it, there *were* signs of things getting slightly run-down. The pickup, for example, had badly needed new rings and tyres. There were a stack of papers on the desk that Louise had evidently been poring over. I looked away from them and lit a cigarette.

'This was supposed to be a gold mine,' I said. 'Are you telling me it's turning out a flop?'

'No. But we've got problems and you're not helping. I can smell the liquor on your breath and...'

That's what I mean about the space being too small for a fight. For the first time I noticed the marks of real worry on her smooth, pretty face and I was touched. She was only a kid really and I wasn't pulling my weight. I flicked the cigarette out the window and came around the desk to touch her. 'What problems, love? Tell me what you mean.'

'I guess you could say she means me, Dick.'

A dark, good-looking man with brilliantined hair, wearing a powder blue suit with a dark blue shirt, tie and display handkerchief, came through the door. It was Johnny Stompanato.

CHAPTER FIVE

ALTHOUGH he went by aliases such as John Steele, John Halliday and even John Valentine, Johnny Stompanato wasn't your regular two-bit guinea hood. He'd been brought up in the mid-west by respectable people but boyhood wildness had taken him to a military school to avoid a juvenile police record. He'd served in the marines in the Pacific in the closing stages of the war and that was the last honest and honourable dollar he'd earned. He'd managed bars and a variety of businesses usually financed by money he'd wangled out of women. He'd been married four or five times and had eventually wound up in Hollywood. His only talents were as a gigolo and a strongarm man. He was arrested fairly often and questioned about the large amounts of money he was carrying, but no charges could be made to stick. He worked as a bouncer, money-shifter and debt-collector for Mickey Cohen and other mob guys which gave him a bit of clout. I had hoped that the last time I'd seen him, when I'd paid off my debt, would be the very last.

'What's the matter, Dick? Not pleased to see an old pal?'

I looked at Louise. 'What's he doing here?'

Stompanato took out his display handkerchief, dusted off the edge of the desk and sat down on it. 'Go ahead, babe,' he said, 'tell him.'

Louise was looking at Stompanato as if he was something that had slid under the door. 'The money we borrowed to set the place up, Dick. It seems that Mr Stompanato represents some of the people we borrowed it from.'

'You borrowed money from the mob?'

'No way to talk,' Stompanato said. 'Legitimate finance organisation. All as legal as taking a crap.'

I lit a cigarette and had to work to keep my hands from shaking. 'I'll bet. Love, we might as well close down and hand them the keys.'

Stompanato lifted his hand lazily. His diamond pinkie ring flashed. 'Uh huh. That's not the way it's going to be. Your backers want you to keep on running the joint, make a success of it.'

Louise looked up from the papers on the desk with something like hope shining in her eyes. 'Do you mean that, Mr Stompanato?'

'Sure I mean it.'

'Put it in writing,' I said.

'Dick!'

'The lady's right, Dick. You should watch your mouth. Now I'm here because you're way behind on your note and Mrs Browning couldn't give us any reassurances. But I've taken a good look around the place and I can see its potential. Fine horses you've got. I'm a horse owner myself. I'd like to take a ride sometime.'

It was on the tip of my tongue to ask if he didn't mean he'd like to *take someone* for a ride, but I bit it back. I just puffed on my Chesterfield and looked sceptical.

'You mean you're not going to foreclose?' Louise said.

'Nah. We'll work something out. How about a smoke, Dick?'

I shook one out. He took it and I lit it for him. His dark eyes were as hard as bottle glass; his face was lean and his white teeth shone against his taut, swarthy skin. He was dangerous, especially when he thought he had the upper hand — like now. He was always confident around women anyway, and for the obvious reason. His nickname was 'Oscar' because his penis was reputed to be of the same approximate size as the Academy Award statuette.

'There's just one thing,' Stompanato said, puffing smoke up at the ceiling which gave Louise a chance to look at his smooth, tanned throat. 'The place needs a few big names. You've been around a long time, Dick. See if you can't get a few of the old-timers to drop in for a brush-up on their riding or horseshoe pitching or something. You know what I mean.'

He sauntered out and I desperately wanted to plant my boot in the seat of his well-tailored pants. Not a good idea. Perhaps I could have stood up to him in a fair fight. I'd never heard that he was much good with his fists and, to judge by his manicure, he hadn't been using them in a business sense lately. But with Johnny Stomp there was no guaranteeing that's what you'd get. I hadn't seen any signs of a gun under the smart tailoring, but a switchblade hardly makes a bulge. I watched him go and then moved to the window. His red T-bird, parked where everybody could get a good look at it, was being admired by a young blonde actress who was one of the string of Grable look-alikes hoping to parlay her tiny talent into big money. She was flirting hard and by the look of things that was where her real ability lay.

To my amazement, Louise had taken a packet of filter cigarettes from her purse and lit up. She blew a stream of smoke at me, not expertly, but the cigarette certainly wasn't her first. 'Well, that wasn't as bad as I expected,' she said. 'You'd better get cracking on rounding up Jimmy Dean and some of the veterans. You heard what the man said.'

'Not bad? Not *bad*? I don't what you'd call bad but I'd say it's as bad as it could possibly be. That guy works for Mickey Cohen and christ knows who else. He hasn't got an honest bone in his body.'

'All we need is some breathing space. Once we get everything on a rock solid footing we can re-finance. Pay these people back and get another loan.'

She didn't know what she was saying, of course. The whole point of mob finance is that you can *never* pay it back or the vigorish.

You just get in deeper and deeper until they own you, body and soul. I didn't have the heart to tell Louise about it. I just gave her a tired, man-of-the-world kind of grin. 'You shouldn't smoke. It'll ruin your complexion.'

'I'll stop when we get through this.'

How many times have I heard that? Including from my own mouth. I left the office and watched the rear end of the Thunderbird as it disappeared down the track. No sign of the blonde. I understood now why Lou Kovacs had been so cooperative and Rocky and Tank so nervous. They knew we had mob money behind us and were naturally afraid of mob muscle. So was I.

I saddled up a horse and went for a ride. It was either that or open up a bottle. I'd seen enough of how the mob operated in Chicago in the 30s and all over the country after the war to know that Louise and I were in serious trouble. We weren't in trouble on the same scale as 'Bugsy' Siegel[10] maybe, but even a small piece of that kind of grief is enough. My natural inclination was to grab Louise and whatever money was lying about, jump into the best car at our disposal and head for the border.

But I felt I was getting a bit old for midnight dashes and Mexico has never been lucky for me. Against my instincts, I tried to think things through a little. I didn't know who Johnny Stompanato was fronting for and that was important. If it was Mickey Cohen that wasn't so bad. Mickey was something of a clown who fancied himself as a standup comic. He was vicious all right, but fickle in his viciousness. If you could stay out of his hair long enough he'd forget you. But there were much heavier characters around and they were starting to move in on Hollywood.

As I rode I tried to work out what dirty schemes they might want to push using our school as a front. These were not comforting thoughts. The possibilities were endless — drugs, blackmail, vice. Taking a powder began to seem like the best option again, but perhaps not straightaway. I began to shape a plan. the first thing was to get Louise on side, then set about putting together some money...

The roar of the motorcycle engine spooked my horse and I had to struggle to keep from being thrown. I was on a quiet road, almost a country track, and there had been no motor traffic in twenty minutes. The bike roared past, swerving to avoid me and bucking when it hit rough patches. It skidded on a sandy stretch and the rider barely pulled out of it. My horse was rearing and snorting. I pulled its head around and galloped after the motorcycle, not expecting to catch up with it, just intending to let the horse run the tension and fright out. After a hundred yards or so the road bent sharply to the left and another skid mark showed that the hot-shot had barely kept his bike in control around that one. The dust he'd thrown up was still hanging in the air.

The horse was calmer now but I was interested to see what happened to the rider — whether he came off before he hit a tree — and I urged it on, following the still audible sound of the engine. The road dropped suddenly and the tracks showed that the bike must have come over the hump and sailed through the air for a good few yards before hitting ground again. Another frantic struggle to retain control, but no drop in speed. The tread straightened out at last and ran up the hill. To judge by the noise, the bike's powerful motor wouldn't be troubled. The horse still seemed eager so went up it at a good clip. I reined in at the top where the road flattened out and the first thing I saw was the big silver and black motor cycle lying on its side with the rear wheel still spinning.

The second thing was a dog, standing by the side of the road barking at a man in leather jacket and jeans who was trying to drag himself upright to stand on a leg that wouldn't support him. He collapsed into the dirt and started to laugh. I rode up and dismounted. It was James Dean. His jeans were torn and blood was running from a gash below the knee that was poking through the rent. His face and hands were scratched and bloody. He was a mess. He looked up at me and a hysterical note entered the cackling laugh.

'Goddamn dog,' he said. 'Almost killed m'self 'count of a goddamn dog.'

His voice was more than usually slurred because he was very, very drunk. I could smell the wine on his breath and the way his eyes were wandering around in his head, refusing to focus, was another familiar sign.

'You badly hurt?' I asked. 'Apart from the knee?'

'Don't think so.' He squinted, trying to get me to hold still. 'Don't I know you?'

'Dick Browning. You're lucky you're not dead the way you were riding.'

The police siren wailed briefly then shut down.

'Jesus,' Dean said. 'Bastards must've come up on another road. Thought I'd lost 'em back there.'

'You're out-running a speed cop?'

'Have to, man. On account of I am stoned like you wouldn't believe as well as drunk.' He dug into the pocket of his jacket, pulled out a Bull Durham pouch and shoved it into my hand. 'Stick this away someplace and give me a cigarette.'

I was so surprised and, I suppose, impressed, by the way he was pulling himself together by an effort of will, that I did what he said. He was puffing furiously as the police black and white came fast from the other direction, stopping in a showy skid.

'Wise ass,' Dean said. He closed his eyes and all the colour went from his face. He pulled himself up into a sitting position and clicked his fingers at the dog. 'Here, boy. C'mon here. C'mon, you stupid fuckin' mongrel.'

Everything seemed to happen at once. First, the motor cycle engine died, then the cop was standing over Dean, casting nervous glances at the dog and not knowing what the hell to do about me and the horse. He was young, not much over twenty and Dean, looking through his long eyelashes with a chalk-white face covered in dust and blood, had his measure in a split second.

'I c... clocked you at seventy-five back there on the highway.'

'You sure it was me, officer?'

The cop licked his lips and glanced across at the bike, then back to his car where another older cop stood leaning on the open door. 'Sure I am. I saw the licence number on that there Harley, plain as day.'

'An' what would that be, that number?'

Dean gave me a look that was partly amusement, partly a plea to play along. He was a piece of work all right, and I had to admire his performance. Besides, I'm no cop lover myself. The dog chose that moment to get into the act by sidling close and licking some blood from Dean's outstretched hand.

I'd put the Bull Durham pouch in my pocket and I shoved my fist in after it and held it there. 'Could I say something, officer? This young man certainly wasn't speeding when he passed me a little way back. And I saw him swerve to avoid hitting the dog. That's why he came off.'

Dean nodded and took a long draw on his cigarette. He turned his head to politely blow the smoke away from the policeman. Then he gave that tired, how-could-you-do-anything-but-love-me smile that seemed to work with both women and men. Some men. The young cop wasn't immune. In a way, everyone in Hollywood is an actor and the cop could see the way the scene was playing. He hitched his gunbelt and cleared his throat.

'Well, I reckon you've learned your lesson. Not bad hurt, are you?'

Dean bravely shook his head. He was too good an actor to bite his lip as well.

'Keep the speed down.' The cop bent to pat the dog which snarled at him. He stepped back quickly and strode off towards his car.

Dean watched him solemnly and didn't laugh until the black and white had backed up and gone the way it had come. I took the pouch out of my pocket and opened the drawstring. One sniff was enough. I tossed it to Dean who caught it deftly, unzipped a pocket in his jacket and tucked it away. He ground out his cigarette in the dirt and shot a worried look at his bike.

'Well, I almost made it. My place is just a long spit from here. But I certainly owe you one, Dick.'

'I reckon you do. And there's a way you can repay me.'

CHAPTER SIX

THE long spit turned out to be a quarter of a mile and we got there by changing our methods of transport. I helped Dean up onto the horse and I chugged along quietly on the scratched but otherwise undamaged motorcycle, keeping it in first gear and ignoring his jibes and catcalls. I hadn't ridden a motorbike in thirty years and had never been near one as powerful as this thing. It felt like being strapped to a doodle-bug,[11] and the thought of getting it up to seventy-five miles an hour was terrifying. I concluded that Dean either wanted to die young or believed that he couldn't be killed at all. Insane, whichever way it was.

His house had about a half acre of garden around it or what could have been garden if anybody had spent any time in it. As it was, the space was rapidly turning back into grassy scrub which was probably how Dean liked it, being a farm boy from Marion, Indiana. I parked the motorbike alongside another of the same breed that seemed to be lacking certain parts and helped Dean down from the horse. He hobbled across to look at the bike, nodded, bummed another cigarette and semi-reluctantly invited me in for a drink. I thought he was already working on ways to escape his obligation to me. I tethered the horse where it could do some useful work in the garden and went up the rough wooden steps into the house.

It was a kind of hunting lodge arrangement — one big room with exposed timber beams and a pine plank floor. There was very little furniture — a few rough bookshelves, half-filled, a table and a couple of mis-matched chairs, a double bed, a few Indian rugs. Very masculine. The kitchen was at one end of the room and consisted of no more than a sink, a wood block bench and a refrigerator. The place was surprisingly neat and I concluded that Dean either wasn't the lazy slob he made himself out to be or that he had a cleaning woman. He opened the fridge and took out a quart jug of white wine.

'This do?' He was back with the slurred mumble, sounding drunk again.

'Sure. I'll fix it. Why don't you do something about those cuts and grazes? Could get infected.'

He nodded and pushed aside a curtain which shielded the bathroom. I heard water running and then a steady stream of curses as he worked on his injuries. The wine was rough but there was a set of very expensive glasses sitting on a shelf above the sink. I poured myself a glass which I drank straight off and then filled two glasses and took them to the table. Dean came out with his hair slicked back, his face still damp and a wet handtowel that he used to clean the wound on his leg and dab at the blood on his hands. He drank his wine straight down and I re-filled the glass. He'd torn his jeans still more to get at the cut and the denim flapped around his skinny shank. He looked more like a fucked-up rodeo rider than a movie star, but I guess that was what he was aiming at.

I took out my Chesterfields and offered him one but he shook his head. 'Got a carton of Luckies about here someplace.'

He hobbled over to the bookshelf and found the carton tucked between a couple of paperbacks. He took two packets, stuffed one in his shirt pocket and ripped the other open with his thumbnail. He had just too many gestures to be real and I expected him to find a wax match next and light it on the same nail. He didn't. He limped back to the table and accepted the flame of my Zippo. He drew the smoke in deeply and took a long pull on his glass. Then he took out another cigarette and rolled the last inch or so in his fingers until the tobacco fell out. He opened the pouch and stuffed the marijuana into the end of the cigarette which he laid by, ready for use. He was a high toxic little son of a bitch, no doubt about that.

'Contract with Warners is lousy,' he mumbled, apparently speaking to the table top. 'Nine pictures in six years. Fucking wienie factory. Lousy money and they got these clauses 'bout my behaviour — drinking, fast driving and such. Treatin' me like I was a kid.'

'Looks like I did you a bigger favour than I thought,' I said. 'A drunk driving charge plus possession of marijuana wouldn't go down too well with Jack L. and the boys.'[12]

'That's a fact.' He laughed. 'That sure is a fact. Well, all's well that ends well. Hey, that's three wells in the one sentence. How about that?'

'Maybe you should be a writer.'

'I couldn't be any worse than some of the writers they got around here. Lousy directors, too.'

I'd never met a successful actor who didn't think he could write better than the writers, direct better than the directors and produce better than the producers. Plus fuck better than any of them. I drank my wine, smoked my cigarette and didn't say anything. We sat in silence for a while. Dean seemed to be mulling something over. He was muttering to himself, smoking jerkily and drinking fast. I began to wonder if he'd taken a knock on the head his behaviour was so peculiar. Eventually, he looked up and grinned. 'Sure fooled that cop, didn't we, Dick? I was trying to remember where I met you and I finally got it — at that dude ranch where you bawled me out for riding my cycle near your horses.'

He pronounced it 'sickle' the way every kid did after a song about a crazy biker made the hit-parades.[13] I can't remember what Brando said in *The Wild One*, probably because he mumbled even worse than James Dean did. This was the first time I witnessed a peculiarity of Dean's — when he was trying to remember something or work out what to say, he muttered to himself as if clearing his head of mental debris and rehearsing. It was very disconcerting until you got used to it. He seemed pleased to have placed me and to reward himself he lit up the marijuana cigarette, took a deep drag and offered it to me. I refused.

'I've got enough vices I can't afford without taking on any more. How come you're riding around high as a kite at this time of day? Shouldn't you be out signing autographs or making a bubble gum commercial or something?'

He let go one of those hissing, cackling laughs ending in a coughing fit. He'd smoked the marijuana by now and was working on the tobacco part of the cigarette, taking deep drags and pulling the smoke right down. As soon as he recovered from the paroxysm he took in more smoke as if he couldn't wait to finish the cigarette and light up another. His fingers were deeply nicotine-stained and his lungs must've been about the same shade as Louis Armstrong. I'm a smoker myself, but I fiddle with them a lot and usually don't smoke them down more than half way. Dean seemed intent on keeping the American Tobacco Company's share price sky high.

'You're a funny guy,' he said when he had some breath to spare for talking. 'You know what a fucked-up business movie acting is, right?'

I nodded. 'It can be. Depends on how you handle it. Bob Hope's done all right.'

'Bob Hope! Guy never acted once in his life. I'm talking about art, man. I'm talking about the craft of acting. I'm talking history — Shakespeare, and the Greeks and the fuckin' Romans.'

We were back to the Greeks and Romans again. Everything seems to go back to them somehow. I let Dean rant and rave and smoke and drink while I looked around his glorified cabin. Usually you an tell a lot about a man by the way he chooses to live and the possessions he has. Not so with Jimmy Dean — he might *genuinely* be interested in the plays of someone called Bertold Brecht and enjoying sharpening a bowie knife on a whetstone, or it might all be a pretence. I never found out for sure and I doubt if anyone did. The thing was, he never quite went too far — didn't roll his own cigarettes, not with tobacco anyway, and didn't spit on the floor. He dabbed at his cuts with the cloth and blew a cloud of smoke so thick it almost made me cough.

'So, how can I help you, Dick? Admitting my debt to you and all as I do.'

Hollywood operates on a series of networks. No one could possibly know everything that's going on, so what people do is tap in to a couple of the networks that most concern them and hope they won't miss out on anything important. To agents like Lou Kovacs and guys like Rocky Graziano, where the mob was putting its money and who the enforcers were was vitally important to decisions they had to make. To someone like Dean, it was more important to know who was screwing who and who was hot and who was not. It was unlikely that he'd ever heard of Johnny Stompanato. I told him that I'd consider it a favour if he showed some interest in our establishment and dropped a positive remark or two about it in the right places. He was only too happy to agree and seemed relieved that I hadn't asked for something tougher.

'Matter of fact,' he said. 'I really could do with some riding lessons and all that, considering the next piece of shit they're going to have me working on.'

'What's that?'

'Ever hear of a book called *Giant*? '

'The best seller? Sure. My wife read it. Said it was great. I haven't read it myself.'

'Don't bother. It's a pile of crap, but it's going to be bigger than *Gone with the Wind* blah, blah, blah. Guess who's in it, along with yours truly James Byron Dean?'

I tried to remember what Louise had told me about the story as she was reading it. Something to do with a cattle baron and his wife. 'How about Henry Fonda and Bette Davis?'

He shrieked with laughter and stamped his feet on the floor until his sore leg made him stop. Tears ran down his cheeks, whether from amusement or because his leg hurt or because he was drunk I couldn't tell.

'No, sir. They're actors! What we're getting is *stars*, don't worry about acting. We're getting Rock Hudson and Elizabeth Taylor.'

'Bit young aren't they? I seem to remember Louise saying it's a three generation story, that book.'

'Doesn't matter. They'll age 'em up. Have to age me some too. I go from my twenties to my forties or thereabouts. No problem, I feel forty sometimes.'

You don't act it, I thought. But I kept my mouth shut. He went on a while about the absence of talent in Hudson and Taylor and how lousy the script was until I began to feel bored. 'Why're you doing it then? You must have some say in what you do?'

'Not much, but the truth is I wanna do it because George Stevens[14] is directing. You see *A Place in the Sun*?'

I nodded. I'd thought it a bit slow and heavy but it had won Stevens the Oscar for directing.

'He got a brilliant performance out of Monty Clift,' Dean said. 'He's gotta be good. Maybe the picture won't be so bad.' He stared at the floor and seemed to be thinking that over, then he suddenly lifted his head. 'Say Dick, the location work's going to be in Texas. How about you come on down there and help out with the horses and cows and all? I reckon I could fix it.'

CHAPTER SEVEN

DON'T ever let anyone tell you James Dean wasn't smart. He was a natural-born sizer-up of situations and manipulator of people. Here he was, within minutes of agreeing to do something he probably didn't want to do much to discharge an obligation, and he was already turning the tables. Trying to reverse or at least square the obligation. I laughed it off at the time and suggested that Dean might be able to get Rock and Liz to visit Sherman House as well as himself and really give the place a push along. He'd considerably lowered the level in the jug by this time and his eyes were dropping. He looked as if he might just have enough energy to make it to the bed.

'Yeah, maybe I could do that. Maybe we could have a barbecue over there. Get Tennessee Ernie Ford and Burl Ives along. Something like that.'

I knew when I was being had and I was determined to get the last word in. I got up from the table and pointed a finger at him. 'Just one thing, Jimmy — no motorcycles.'

He grinned at me. 'I kinda enjoyed riding that horse. Might travel that way from now on.'

Then I said something I've never forgotten. 'You should get yourself a car.'

'I got a car. I got me a Porsche roadster.'

'I mean a real car,' I said, meaning a Ford or a Buick, even a Cadillac.

Dean rubbed the graze on his chin. "Maybe I'll do that. Maybe I will.'

Back at Sherman House, I gave Louise an edited version of my encounter with Dean, leaving out the drugs and not mentioning the idea of my working on *Giant* because I hadn't taken that seriously. I told her that Jimmy said he'd bring Rock and Liz to a barbecue, meaning it as a joke. Louise, who normally could see a joke as quickly as anyone, was too worried to let her sense of humour work. She seized on it.

'Oh, Dick, that's marvellous! That could really turn things around here.' She kissed me hard and pressed herself against me in a way she had that always caused me to lose the thread of what I was thinking. I kissed her back and before we knew it we were reconciling like crazy on the living-room rug. After that, I didn't have the heart to tell her that her plans were pipe-dreams and that once the mob got a hold they never let go. You could get too big in Hollywood for the gangsters to be able to give you any grief — people like Zanuck and Goldwyn and Tracey and Hepburn, Parsons and Hopper[15] were like that, but Louise and I and Sherman House were never going to climb that high.

I got the first whiff of trouble within a week. I was on the court giving a tennis lesson to a girl whose breasts were so large she couldn't hit a proper groundstroke without them getting in the way. It was a novel problem for a tennis coach and I was trying to figure a way around it when I noticed a grey Dodge coupe come up the road and park in the shade of a stand of eucalypts. The driver got out and for a minute I didn't know who he was because he wasn't dressed as if he was going to a garden party. He wore dark pants and a plain jacket, but the jaunty way he whipped off his sunglasses and stowed them in his pocket was familiar. He beckoned me with an arrogant wave and that's when I recognised Stompanato.

I made a point of completing the instruction I was giving.

'On the forehand, Sally, you'd do better to take the ball on the rise. Hit it a bit earlier and benefit from the pace that's already on it. Try hitting your backhand double-handed, like this.'

'Why?'

I knew what she wanted me to say — because that might get your great big beautiful tits out of the way. I didn't. I hit two balls in demonstration, both perfect strokes as it happened, patted balls at her and watched while she tried to do the same.

'Better,' I said, although it wasn't. 'Keep practising and excuse me for a minute.'

'Nice jugs,' Stompanato said through the mesh fence.

'Thought you might notice. Here for your riding lesson?'

'I don't need lessons from you at anything, Dick. Let's get that straight. No, I got a guest for you.'

'We don't take guests, just fee-paying students.'

Stompanato laughed. 'You'll take this one. I want you to put him in one of the cabins, far as possible out of sight. He'll need meals, booze, maybe a broad if he wants one. Like that.'

I shook my head. 'The cabins're all full. Try again next week.'

Stompanato gripped the mesh. I noticed that he wasn't wearing his diamond ring and that he hadn't shaved for a day or so. His eyes were red-rimmed and his breath smelled of booze and tobacco. Normally he was fastidious about those things. 'Listen, Browning, I'm not asking you I'm telling you. Which means other people are telling you, understand?'

Of course I understood. I glanced across at the Dodge and could just make out the shape of a person sitting in the back. 'Who is he?'

He was still tense, still gripping the fence, and the laugh he gave was more nervous than amused. 'Don't ask. Don't think about it.'

'Mr Browning!' Well-endowed Sally was calling me from the centre of the court. She'd run out of balls.

'It'll take a while to arrange,' I said. 'An hour or so.'

Stompanato glanced at his watch. 'We'll drive around. Be back in one hour exactly. Be ready!'

Louise was off on a trail ride so I made the arrangements myself — moved one of the cabin dwellers into the house and left him a note saying we'd lower his fees. He wouldn't like it because he was romancing one of the actresses but he'd have to put up with it. The cabin I allotted to the mystery man was the furthest from the house, situated in a little clutch of pine trees. It was private but not the most comfortable of the out-buildings — there were squirrels in the roof and the place leaked on the rare occasions that it rained. I got some satisfaction out of that.

The Dodge cruised along, looking like the sort of car a country doctor might drive. Stompanato stopped where I was standing, got out and took a suitcase from the trunk. His passenger climbed from the back seat. He was short and slight, wearing a grey suit, wide-brimmed hat and large-lensed, very dark sunglasses. The suit didn't quite fit him, and from the way he stood it looked as if the nondescript black brogues weren't such a good fit either.

'This is Mr Lewis,' Stompanato said. 'Where's the accommodation?'

I pointed. Johnny Stomp picked up the suitcase and indicated with a jerk of his head that I should lead the way. I took the track that ran behind the stables; although there were other ways to get to the cabin, this was the most private. I didn't look at Stompanato's companion for one second longer than I needed to. It was probably my imagination, but he seemed to chill the mild Californian air. I stepped up onto the porch to the cabin and heard the wheezing breath coming from Mr Lewis as he followed. We hadn't walked more than a hundred yards, — not a well man.

I waited outside while the two of them looked the cabin over. It had two bedrooms and the basic facilities, no luxuries but no cockroaches or bed bugs.

'It's a dump,' I heard Stompanato say.

'It'll do fine. It ain't for long. Give the guy his instructions and tell him to blow. I wanna have a rest.'

I can hear that voice to this day — it was thin and reedy with a touch of Italian under the accent of the Lower East side of New York. You could tell that the man was used to being obeyed instantly. He was one of those people who wield so much power they can't actually have any conversations. They just talk and someone jumps. Stompanato came out onto the porch and lit a cigarette.

'Mr Lewis'll be here for a few days, a week maybe. He'll have visitors and he'll make some trips. None of this is any fuckin' business of yours or of the fruits and broads you got around here. I'll be with him some of the time and when I'm not here there'll be someone else. Is the phone connected to the house?'

I nodded.

'We want, you bring. Got it?'

'What do I tell my wife?'

'You tell her if she doesn't do exactly what she's told your note gets called in, or maybe the place gets torched, or some horses break their legs. Whatever it takes to keep her in line.'

'A week?'

Stompanato scowled and flicked his butt into a pile of pine needles not far from the cabin. I jumped down and went across to put my boot on the smouldering butt.

'That's a good way to send Mr Lewis straight to hell, Johnny.'

Stompanato's snake eyes bored into me. 'Shut your stupid mouth. That ain't funny. Go get my bag from the Dodge and bring it here. Then wait till you're wanted.'

I walked back to the car, mentally running through the accidents I'd like to happen to Johnny Stompanato. What troubled me most was the sense I had that Johnny Stomp was scared of the man he was bodyguarding, and if *he* was scared, I was terrified.

'But who *is* he?' Louise asked, puffing furiously on a cigarette.

'I don't know and I don't want to know. Some kind of gangster who's hiding out, sort of.'

She snorted derisively. 'What kind of an answer's that? I'm going right over there and find out what this is all about.'

We were standing just inside the door of our house where I'd grabbed Louise as she was on the way to the shower and given her the bad news. Like any good North Shore girl, she didn't like to hang around all hot and sweaty, but she meant what she said and moved towards the door. I gripped her arm hard enough to make it hurt.

'Listen to me, love. If you don't do exactly what Stompanato says, I'm almost certainly a dead man. You could get your face rearranged and when he says that this place could get torched he means it. He'd enjoy doing all three things, or having them done.'

'This is insane. Let me go!'

'Not until you promise you won't go near that cabin.'

'How will I explain it to Joe and Patty? What will they think?' These were the lovebirds, rapidly moving into battle stations with each other.

'I've given Joe the second best room in the house. The french windows make it semi-private. I've left him a note saying I'll drop his fees. It doesn't matter what people think just what they do! This is our place. What we say goes.'

She stared at me and I realised the stupidity of what I'd just said. I shrugged. 'It can't be helped. It's only for a week.'

She banged her riding hat with her fist. Louise could give quite a bang and the hat dented. 'And then what? What will it be next time? A whole car load of hoods taking over the house?'

Easily, I thought. *Or worse.* I shrugged again and let go of her arm before she decided to put a dent in me.

'All right,' she said. 'We'll do what you say, but we'll have to get something out of this ourselves. Doing this has to count for something.'

'You don't bargain with the mob, Louise. You do what they say or else. If you get real lucky someone rubs out the people who're giving you a hard time and then you get left alone. That's the best outcome you can expect.'

'Is it? That's ridiculous. We'll see about that. Give me a cigarette.'

I gave her a Chesterfield and lit it. She puffed on it like a serious smoker. She graduated quickly from the filters. I watched her as she got herself under control and a look I'd come to know came into her eyes. It was a combination of calculation and stubbornness, very worrying in the present circumstances.

'What've you got in mind? Don't cross these guys. There's no percentage in it.'

'Like I say, we'll see. This tastes disgusting. I'm not going to do this anymore.' She dropped the butt into a pot plant and I never saw her smoke a cigarette again. Louise fully determined was a scary sight. It was my day for being frightened all right. But it was too serious to let her have the last word and I reached for her again. She skipped away, eluding me easily.

'Louise! This is life and death. What're you planning to do.'

She was heading for the stairs. 'I'm going to get a lawyer.'

I let her go. I had to. I was laughing too hard to do anything else.

CHAPTER EIGHT

THE next week at Sherman House should have been a disaster, with a man hiding out in one of the cabins, being served his meals, coming and going in his dark glasses and receiving visitors at dead of night, and the paying students being re-shuffled and told nothing about the new arrangements. Throw in the nervousness of the manager and his wife's agitation over everything and you have a recipe for a colossal fuck-up. But we got lucky. All these disruptions were over-shadowed by the news that Jimmy Dean was bringing Rock Hudson and Elizabeth Taylor to a weekend barbecue. It was all anyone could talk about and the arrangements necessary to make it a success absorbed Louise and soaked up even her reserves of energy.

I kept an eye on Mr Lewis, figuratively speaking. In fact, I never saw him. There was a kitchen in the cabin so Stompanato or the other bodyguards were able to take care of most of the food requirements. When something was required from the house, I was the one who delivered it and then only as far as the porch. That suited me. I was careful not to look at any of the late night visitors if I happened to be around when they arrived, or to pay any attention to their cars. A worry to me was that our guest or his visitors or both threw their cigar butts out of the cabin windows. I made a point of putting a fire extinguisher at the front and back doors. The next time I looked there were no more cigar butts. With gangsters, actions speak louder than words.

Still, I was nervous. A police siren could make me jump and a backfiring engine almost had me diving for cover. The standard of my teaching fell off badly, but the students put it down to excitement over the visit of the stars. If only they knew. I'd seen too many stars drunk and incapable, cheating at games, pleading for another chance, chiselling and penny-pinching to have any illusions about that species. When Dean telephoned me with the glad tidings, the first thing I did was check that Hudson and Taylor were actually in town. They were, so Jimmy's story had a chance of being true. But in Hollywood you can't be sure a star you're expecting has arrived until you hand him or her the first drink. I told Louise not to get her hopes up too high. I don't think she even heard me. She wasn't star-struck herself, she was simply seeing it as a possible way out of the financial hole. Me, I was just glad of the distraction.

The bill for the steaks and salads and rolls must have come to a couple of hundred bucks plus the outlay for beer, wine and liquor. Louise was making a big investment in Jimmy Dean's credibility. Stompanato wasn't happy when I told him about the gala event, but he knew Hollywood and that, no matter how much clout Mr Lewis had, Rock Hudson and Elizabeth Taylor outranked him.

'Maybe Mr Lewis would like to meet them,' I suggested. 'You know, get their autograph for Mrs Lewis and the kids.'

'That smart mouth of yours is going to get you dead one day,' was all he said.

The great day dawned fine and clear, like three hundred days a year in southern California, and the stars arrived dead on time, accompanied by the usual hangers-on. Hudson was in a two-tone Cadillac convertible, Taylor in a Rolls Royce and James Dean headed the parade as an outrider on his motorcycle with Pier Angeli as his pillion passenger. He grinned as he brought the bike to stop a yard in front of me.

'Thought I'd just kinda ride escort, you know? Seeing as I knew the way and all.'

'I wonder what a pound of sugar in the gas tank would do to it.'

'Now, Dick, didn't I deliver? Aren't those two great stars of the silver screen here to make you and your place famous?'

Hudson was bigger than I expected him to be and Elizabeth Taylor was smaller. Louise wasn't over-awed. Before long she had the students cooking steaks and serving drinks — which was what a good few of them had been doing for a living before this anyway — and the event started to go with a swing. Dean hung around on the edges, saying little, eating nothing and drinking steadily. I didn't know what his relationship with Pier Angeli was like in general, but that day they seemed to be barely on speaking terms. She flirted with the students, he glowered. Some of the students tried to talk to him about acting but he froze them out. They expected it and his behaviour didn't dampen the proceedings.

Hudson was quietly spoken and polite. He seemed a little bored by the company and not at all interested in horses or the outdoor life. He resembled a cattle baron the way a duck resembles a donkey. Elizabeth Taylor was queenly as if she was getting ready to play Cleopatra which she did a few years later. Some of the students got drunk and one broke his leg falling off a horse. He was one of the worst riders I'd ever seen and I was impressed that he'd even managed to get up on the horse. He couldn't do it sober.

Louise had made sure the newspapers were represented and she took care that the reporters got their share of the food and drink as well as a chance to pick up a few quotes from the stars. Hudson said that Sherman House was 'mighty fine'; Taylor said it was 'charming' and Jimmy Dean just grunted. Taylor put on a Texas accent and said, 'Now Jett, you jus' be more polite, you hear?'

Dean grinned, mimed pulling off his hat and said, 'This place you got here, Mr Browning, why it's mighty fine and charming.'

Smiles all round with Hudson and Taylor dimly aware that they'd been sent up. They left pretty soon after, taking Pier Angeli and their entourage with them. Dean was very drunk by this time.

He'd taken off his leather jacket and was arm-wrestling with one of the students. I took the motorbike keys out of the jacket and prepared myself for one of those encounters you have with drunks who want to drive home when they can barely stand. Dean lost the match, had another drink and reissued the challenge. I went up to the house to phone the hospital for a report on the broken leg.

I stepped into the office and found Stompanato there, talking urgently into the phone. It took me a second or two to register that he was speaking in Italian.

'What the hell are you doing?'

He whipped around, barked a few words into the phone and hung up. He was too deeply tanned to turn pale but he was clearly very agitated. So was I when he pulled out a gun and pointed it at me. I shook my head and sort of waved at the pistol with my hands, gesturing for him to lower it or point it somewhere else. He must have misinterpreted my action, or maybe he was just worked up. Anyway, he stepped closer and jabbed me in the ribs with the business end. I gasped at the sudden pain and for a second I thought I'd been shot. Stompanato swept the gun up, getting set to swipe me across the skull with it. I crouched and tilted myself away but I was slow and I knew it. Then he stopped the action. It sounds strange but in that moment of acute fear I actually *saw* him change his mind.

'Browning,' he said. 'Fucking Browning, you came along just at the right time.' He pointed to the sets of car keys hanging on hooks on a board. 'What's the best heap you've got?'

I almost pissed myself with relief. If he wanted to take a car he could have his pick. 'The Buick, goes like a rocket.'

'Grab the keys and come with me. Do everything I say or I'll shoot you, I swear it.'

I took the keys and he ushered me out with nervous, jerky movements of the gun. The barbecue was still going on but we were shielded from it by the stables. Stompanato jabbed me again. 'Bring the Buick as close as you can to the cabin, and make it quick.'

I broke into a run and he ran off towards the cabin. I think he was the only gangster I ever saw run anywhere. Most of them got their exercise walking between cars and bar stools. As I got to the garage I heard the crackle of gunfire coming from somewhere not too far off. That speeded me up. I had the Buick started, backed and roaring towards the track that led to the cabin in record time. I saw Stompanato and Mr Lewis hurrying through the trees, Stompanato carrying a suitcase and Lewis hanging on to his hat and gasping for breath. I pulled up and opened the door. Stompanato shoved the pistol in my ear.

'You're driving,' he said.

He threw the suitcase in the backseat and almost threw Lewis in after it. The man's breath was coming in short, wheezing gasps and he was cursing softly and steadily in Italian.

'Where're we going?'

'Take that old road, the one you don't use.'

'It's mostly pot holes, we'll bust a spring or an axle.'

'Don't bust nothin'. Just do it.'

To get onto the dirt road, disused for years before I had taken over the property, I had to pass close to the festivities. I saw Louise glance towards us as I shot by. God knows what she was thinking. I didn't see Dean and I hoped that he'd passed out. It was going to be hard explaining where the keys to his 'sickle' were. Funny the things you think about when your life's in danger. The road was as rough as I'd said and I had to drop speed to negotiate it. I could feel Stompanato's impatience but he could see that I knew what I was doing and he kept quiet. He chain-smoked and I could smell the rich aroma of a Havana cigar coming from the back seat.

We came out on a back road and I stopped and set the emergency brake.

'What d'you think you're doin'?' Stompanato growled.

'You just needed me back there. You can take it from here.'

He jabbed me again in the same spot. 'No dice. Get goin'. South.'

I drove in silence for several miles, heading towards San Diego. There's not much to see on that drive — hills, towns, beach, more hills, more towns, more beaches. The traffic was light. I kept within the speed limit which meant that a lot of cars passed me. Stompanato didn't comment so I figured I was doing the right thing. On the outskirts of San Diego I had to stop for gas and I needed to piss.

'Don't get funny ideas about writing on the mirror with soap,' Stompanato said as he got out with me and sauntered along towards the door marked 'Men'. 'Just get back here quick.'

Of course I hadn't had anything so heroic in mind. My idea was simply to jump out a window and run. But there wasn't a window and Johnny was waiting for me when I came out. He escorted me back to the car. The guy who'd pumped the gas was standing around with his hand out and I paid him. Quite by accident I looked into the back seat as I accepted my change. The light was falling in the right way and I got my first and only clear look at Mr Lewis. I almost blacked out. I'll swear my knees sagged. Stompanato didn't notice and I climbed into the car with my hands and every part that could shake shaking. The man in the back seat was Lucky Luciano.[16]

CHAPTER NINE

LUCKY Luciano, 'Charley Lucky', top man in the Syndicate whether he was in exile in Italy or hanging around Cuba, even when he was in gaol. God alone knew how many men he'd put under the ground before they were ready to go. He was supposed to be in Italy where he'd been deported after the war, and now he was riding in the back seat of my car. It felt like playing chauffeur to Adolf Hitler if your name was Izzy Bernstein. Fear almost froze me but I managed to keep moving, get the car started and pull out of the gas station onto the road. I had tunnel vision and a roaring in my ears. It was lucky there was no other car coming along because I was scarcely aware of what I was doing.

There was no mistake. Plenty of pictures of him had been published, mostly with him wearing dark glasses as he was now. But I remembered that I'd seen him once before, in Chicago in the old days when I was hanging around night-clubs, spending money on heartless women.[17] Twenty-five years on and he was smaller and greyer of skin but I'd caught a glimpse just now of those scars on his neck he'd got in a knife fight when he was a crime apprentice. It was a mild day but I wanted to shiver as I smelled the rich cigar smoke coming from the back seat. Stompanato had taken the passenger's seat and was turned around, saying something in Italian in a low voice. A hundred things ran through my mind, none of them cheerful. I couldn't think of a single reason why they wouldn't

PETER CORRIS

bump me off when I stopped being useful. That was what I had to focus on — I had to come up with a reason.

In the meantime it was crucial that they didn't know I'd identified Mr Lewis. I wound down the window a little more to dry the sweat on my hands and face and screwed up my courage to be old brash Dick Browning.

'Say, Johnny, give me a cigarette will you?'

'Smoke your own.'

'I feel like a change. Don't you ever change brands? You ever think of quitting?'

'Why?'

Good question. In the gangster business you might as well have every vice you can manage because you probably won't be around long to enjoy them.

The voice from the back was as cold as a meat locker. 'Give the guy a cigarette and tell him to shut up. I wanna catch some sleep.'

Stompanato gave me one of his Camels and I lit it with the dash lighter. 'Same brand as James Dean,' I whispered.

He looked vaguely interested. 'Yeah?'

'Right. He was at the party. You should have dropped by to meet him and Rock and Liz.'

'Fuck 'em.'

'Interesting thought.'

'When I said shut up I meant both of you. You driving, you talk funny. Where you from?'

'Australia originally, Mr Lewis.'

'They talk English down there?'

'Yes sir, they do.'

'Well shut the fuck up!'

No question but he was addressing the two of us and we both went dead quiet until we heard the sound of soft snoring. I waited until the rhythm of the snores indicated deep sleep before I spoke.

'Where are we going, Johnny?'

58

'The border, Mexico, where else?'

'Then what?'

Stompanato turned slightly in his seat to look more directly at me. For one horrible instant I thought he might have realised that I'd recognised the passenger, but he just wanted to let me get the full force of his scorn.

'What in hell could make you think I'm giving the fucking orders around here?'

I chewed that over on the rest of the drive from San Diego to Tijuana. I've never much cared for Mexico, but Tijuana isn't Mexico. I remember Raymond Chandler telling me that one time when I said I was going down there for the horse races.

'It's a border town,' Chandler said, 'and a border town is just a border town. It isn't really anywhere except where it is.'

He used to talk like that and I never quite understood him. Maybe it makes more sense written down. I wouldn't know, I've never read any of his books. Anyway, in those days, if you were white and driving an American registered car, you could come and go across the border and no one would bother you. Occasionally a border guard might ask to look in the trunk, but that was really just a way of bumming a pack of cigarettes or squeezing a few bucks out of you. Squeezing money out of Americans was what Tijuana was all about.

Playing at being unconcerned is hard work. For example, you might decide to hum a little tune to show that you've got no worries. On the other hand, mightn't that show nervousness? Or that you're trying too hard? My best chance was for Luciano and Stompanato to think that this was just a little mob sideshow, nothing to get in a sweat over. Never before in my life had I so much wanted to read another man's mind. Did Johnny Stomp know I'd heard the gunfire? That made a difference. And why didn't they have a getaway plan ready for use? Why this improvisation? Of course I'd been keeping an eye out for cops, but Luciano would be a Federal matter and if there's any way to spot FBI agents driving along the public highways I don't know it.

I tensed up as the bridge came in sight but that was only natural. Stompanato was edgy too and Luciano must have woken up because the snoring had stopped.

'How do I play it?' I asked.

'Don't do nothin',' Stompanato said. 'We got guys front and back.'

Ahead of me was a grey Plymouth and in back a blue De Soto — solid, respectable-looking cars just like the Buick. I suppose they had been with us the whole way and I hadn't noticed a thing. Well, my private eye days were long behind me,[18] and I never would have made much of a gangster. We barely got a glance from the border guards and rolled into Mexico as if we had come down for the whores and the tequila and the bullfights just like all the other suckers. A short shower of rain helped, making the guards reluctant to venture out from their shelter. The question for me was, were my troubles over now that we were out of US jurisdiction, or were they just beginning?

I glanced at Stompanato who was chewing his bottom lip and looking almost as nervous as I felt. 'Where to now?'

'The harbour.'

I knew my way around Tijuana pretty well, better, anyway, than the driver of the Plymouth which fell back behind us. By the time the water came in view Stompanato had worried his lip raw. I drew up near the barrier to the main wharf and heard the back door open.

'Wait,' Luciano said as he got out. The rain had stopped and steam was rising from the warm cement.

There were two men in each of the cars, one about as big as me, the others smaller but capable-looking. Luciano joined them by the barrier and began to give orders, pointing here and there and gesturing with his hands.

'I don't like this,' Stompanato said.

'What?'

'I know one of those guys. He'd rather cut a throat than fuck Lana Turner.'

A strange thing for him to say in view of later events, but my memory of the conversation is clear as it is of all the occasions when I thought my last moment had come.

'What're you saying?'

'They'll get us out on the boat and bump us for sure.'

Johnny Stompanato was not the man I'd have chosen to be my ally but right then I'd have taken Don Vito himself.[19] 'Well then, let's get the hell out while we've got the chance.'

'Can't. His bag's still in the trunk. Probably got a hundred grand or so in it. They'd track us to the ends of the earth.'

I couldn't believe it. My survival was going to turn on a little thing like a bag being in a trunk instead of in the car. I looked across at the gangsters. They were perhaps fifty feet away, still in what passed for conversation with Luciano, but at any minute one of them could come across and tell us what to do. Sweat was running freely down Stompanato's face and his hands were trembling. Maybe he'd put men in cement shoes himself in his time and he knew better than me what to expect.

'Have you got a gun?' I asked.

'Yeah, but you don't pull a gun on...'

'I know who he is.' I'd played my only card and I had nothing to lose now. 'Listen, if I hop out, open the trunk and dump the bag will you fire one shot over their heads?'

'Jeez, I dunno...'

'One shot. Straight up in the air for Christ's sake. I've done stunts like this in the movies. I can do it in about five seconds. We can be out of here inside ten seconds. They don't know the town and I do. We can be back in the States in a couple of minutes and then what can they do? Come on!'

Stompanato gulped but he took out his pistol. 'Ok.'

I knew if I thought about it I'd never have the nerve. I pulled the keys from the ignition, jumped out and sprinted to the back of the Buick. It's amazing how quickly you can react when your life's on the line. I had the trunk key at the ready as soon as I was in reach and slid it smoothly into the lock and turned. The lid jumped up and hit me in the face but I jerked the bag out and slammed the lid down, reaching again for the key. Although I was like a golfer, keeping my head down and concentrating on the shot, I was so pumped up I seemed to have wide angle vision. I saw the knot of men break up, heard voices and had a sense of two of them already on the move towards me.

My brain was screaming: *Shoot! For Christ's sake shoot!* but I didn't waste any breath. I had the key in one hand and the bag in the other. One of the smaller thugs was as quick as a bantamweight; he'd gained a yard on the other one and seemed to be reaching inside his jacket. Again, I didn't think; I swung the bag back and threw it at him, not aiming, just hoping. The bag slammed into his face and he lost balance. The guy behind fell over him and that's when Stompanato fired. I was back in the driver's seat with the sound of the shot still ringing out. Sweat was dripping into my eyes but I got the ignition key in again first time. The motor caught and I was in gear and accelerating with the door still swinging open beside me.

'Go! Go! Go!' Stompanato screamed.

The air filled with the smell of burning rubber and the screech of tortured tyres. The door slammed shut as I threw the Buick around a bend — just as well because the violence of the turn might have slung me out. I gripped the wheel and concentrated on covering as much distance as I could in the shortest possible time. It was close to sunset and there weren't many people around — a few sailors, a few strollers, some street vendors — they scattered like frightened sparrows as I roared down a narrow street, fighting to control the wheels on cobblestones that were greasy with trash and overflow from the gutters.

I almost hit a lumbering, over-loaded bus as I made another turn and Stompanato shouted at me to slow down. He was still holding his gun and for a minute I thought he was going to shoot me. I eased off the gas and concentrated on steering straight and clearing my blurred vision.

'We made it,' I said, after I'd driven along a quiet street for some minutes and checked the rear vision mirror. 'They're not following.'

'Yeah, right.'

'You don't sound too happy about it.'

He put his pistol away and lit a cigarette with hands that trembled violently. 'I fired a shot at Lucky Luciano. I could've signed my death warrant.'

You said it yourself. We were dead men if we'd got on their boat.'

'I need a drink bad. You know a place?' 'Shouldn't we get back across the border?'

'I need it now! Find a bar or somewhere we can get a fucking bottle.'

The idea appealed to me. I drove for a couple of minutes getting my bearings and then headed for a liquor store near the bullring where you could buy whisky that hadn't been watered down too far. Stompanato seemed to be making a deliberate effort to relax. He lit a cigarette, handed me one and lit it with his gold lighter. I started to relax too — a close shave but out of danger with the skin intact. All you could ask. Time to be generous.

I puffed smoke out of the window. 'You fired the shot at just the right time. Really held them up.'

'You did all right, Dick,' he grunted. 'Didn't know you had it in you.'

'Situation like that,' I said, 'you've just gotta do it, not think about it. You were in the marines, you must know.'

'Yeah. I tell you what, I felt safer on Guadalcanal with all them Japs than I did back there with Charley Lucky and his boys.'

He was perking up and making me feel better. 'What was he doing here?'

'Some top level meeting of mob guys. I don't think it went too well. Also, it looks like someone squealed. We had to move fast.'

The bullring was in sight and the liquor store was still in business. I pointed it out to Stompanato. 'What kind of liquor d'you want?'

'Scotch,' he said. 'Park in the alley there. We still gotta be careful'

I pulled into the alley. He moved, I thought he was reaching for his wallet, but what hit me on the side of the head wasn't made of leather and it didn't have money in it.

CHAPTER TEN

W<small>HEN</small> I came to I was sitting in the alley with my back up against a damp wall and my feet in the usual Mexican refuse — cigarillo packets, sugar-cane fibre and broken glass. I couldn't have been there for long because my wallet was still in my pocket and I was still wearing all my clothes — tasselled loafers, slacks, a sport shirt and a cream linen jacket. I was also carrying a headache that was threatening to divide my skull in two. The car had gone, of course, and Johnny Stompanato had left his memento in the shape of a cut above my left ear that dripped blood down into the ear and onto the shoulder of my jacket. I touched the cut with a hesitant finger. Luckily, I still had a head of thick hair which had absorbed some of the impact of the blow and soaked up some of the blood. Still, I wasn't feeling nearly as chipper as I had been a few minutes before.

I pressed back against the wall and slowly levered myself up. The alley spun around a few times, but then it came back to rest in a more or less manageable condition. I took a few tentative steps forward in the direction of the street and didn't fall over. Encouraged, I stood and took out a handkerchief, spat and used it to clean up some of the blood. I was still on my feet and the headache wasn't much worse than with a bad hangover. Maybe it was association of ideas, but the best move at that point seemed to me to get myself into a bar and my hand around a glass of whisky.

I found my way into the bar beside the liquor outlet which had been my original target. More American in decor and service than Mexican, the bar served whisky and beer as well as tequila and white rum, and I took a shot of rye and a stein of draught into a quiet, dark corner as aids to my recovery and to considering my options. Experience had taught me that, when travelling alone in foreign lands, the first and most important question is always: how much money do you have? I had the grand sum of one hundred and twelve dollars. Not bad for Mexico, where at that time you could live pretty well for two dollars a day as long as you didn't mind eating tortillas and drinking rotgut tequila. I'd got used to something better and wasn't comforted.

Something else Raymond Chandler had said came back to me: whisky can make your head feel worse but you feel better. This was more understandable than most of his remarks and I was experiencing the truth of it. The rye was dulling the pain only a little but enabling me to think more clearly and quite fast. The thoughts were not encouraging. I was in trouble. By now, the FBI must know that I had helped Lucky Luciano escape. My dealings with the Feds[20] had convinced me that they were a bunch of insecure prima donnas, incapable of keeping their word for more than twenty-four hours at a stretch. I could expect no mercy from them and, if I was tossed into a Federal prison with the other Mafia hoods, after the part I'd played with Stompanato, my survival chances were lower than a dachshund's knee.

'Another shot and chaser, Senor?'

I must have been slightly concussed. I'd finished my drinks and wandered back up to the bar without realising it. I put the glasses down and stared at myself in the mirror behind the bar. Not too bad — the beginnings of jowls but what can you expect at fifty- five?[21] The hair on one side was crusted with blood and there were stains on the shoulder of my jacket but they're used to that sort of thing in Mexican bars. Their attitude is, if you can stand up and pay you're fit and well.

'No,' I said. 'Telephone. Have you got one?'

He pointed to the end of the bar where the phone sat on top of a stack of US directories. 'Many Americanos come in here,' the barman said. 'Sometimes they forget their telephone numbers. We have the books for Los Angeles, Chicago and New York.'

'That's good thinking,' I said. I put a dollar on the bar and got a fistful of Mexican change. I realised that I was leaving a trail so clear and wide A1 Hibbler[22] could follow it, but I had no choice. I had to assume that Luciano and the boys had boarded their boat and that it would take some time before they sent anyone to remonstrate with me for the rude way I'd treated the boss, if they ever did. I shovelled money into the phone and dialled the number for Sherman House, praying that Louise would answer and not some gung-ho junior G-man. She did.

'Louise, it's me, Dick. Can you talk? Is there a tap on the line?'

'Dick, where in hell are you? Of course I can talk. How would I know if there's a tap on the line? It'd be wonderful if there was.'

'What d'you mean?'

'Dick, it's been so exciting! FBI men running around all over the place. We heard shots. You're not hurt are you?'

Nice of her to ask. As well as aching, my head was now spinning. I was having difficulty believing that I was talking to my wife, my partner in life and the Sherman House Dramatic Skills Academy.

'The FBI men said you helped some gangster escape. They didn't tell me who he was. I showed them the cabin and they put fingerprint dust everywhere and took away a lot of cigar butts.'

'Jesus, Louise. What did you tell them?'

'Nothing, which is what I know. I said there was a Mr Lewis staying there. An elderly gentleman.'

I burst out laughing, drawing a sharp look from the barman and hurting my head. 'They must've loved that — an elderly gentleman. What else?'

'Nothing. They were really very sweet. I think they were relieved that they didn't have to shoot at anyone. Everyone at the party thought it was great. Jimmy was terribly impressed.'

'Jimmy?'

'James Dean of course. He wants you to get in touch with him. Have you got his number?'

This was madness but I didn't know how to stop it. 'No, I haven't got his bloody number.'

'Be nice. Here it is. And this is his number in the valley, not just his paging service.' I snapped my fingers and mimed a writing action to the barman. He whipped a pencil from behind his ear and scribbled on a drink coaster as I called out the numbers.

'Got it,' I said. 'Look, I don't understand any of this. Why are you sounding so chipper?'

'Because this place is already on the way to becoming famous, notorious, whatever you want to call it. We've had the newspaper and radio people around, television too.'

I had to ask the same question. 'What did you tell them?'

The operator came on the line saying something I didn't understand. I put more money in the slot and the line cleared. If she was listening and understood English this was going to make her day.

'I didn't tell them anything at all because I didn't know anything. Mr Silkstein told me that was exactly the right thing to do.'

'You've spoken to Bobby? How did he get into the act?'

'He called me. News like this travels fast. He says we can expect enrolments to double. Dick, are you there? Dick...'

I'd jammed the phone close to my ear and jarred the cut. The pain was intense and tears were seeping from my eyes. The barman looked at me curiously and I signalled for another shot. He brought it quickly and it helped to steady me.

'Listen, Louise, are you saying I can just stroll back home and no one will care?'

'Oh, no, darling. No, you can't do that. Not yet. I'm sure the FBI would do something terrible to you. I told you, they think you helped... '

'I was kidnapped.'

'But you were driving. I saw you.'

'Did you say so?'

'Well, yes, but...'

I groaned and the barman looked inquisitively at me. I shook my head. I had enough trouble without getting pie-eyed. Louise apologised for making me out to be the wheel man but I hardly heard her. I was desperately trying to think of what to do, where to go and how to get there. Nothing came.

Louise must have sensed my desperation because she took over. 'Listen, darling. I'll contact a lawyer and talk to him about your case. Get some advice. You'd better stay in Mexico for a while until I do. I'll wire you some money. Where should I send it?'

I had to laugh. With the FBI and very possibly the mob keen to know my whereabouts she was asking me to provide an address. But the lawyer and the money sounded like good ideas. I told her to send me some cash by mail, addressed to Richard Kelly care of General Delivery, Tijuana, and to make sure no one saw her doing it. I said I'd call her when I'd got the money and figured out my next move. All this had sobered her down and she asked if she shouldn't come down to look after me. She had no idea of how these things worked. I told her no, urged her to see the lawyer and get the business running as hot as she could and to believe less than half of what Bobby Silkstein told her.

She told me she loved me and I had another drink on the strength of that. The barman gave me the drink coaster and I shoved it in my pocket.

CHAPTER ELEVEN

I booked into a small backstreet hotel and set about changing my appearance slightly. It wasn't so difficult. I have a heavy beard and have always been able to present a very respectable growth within five or six days. It used to be dark but a lot of grey had crept in. There was a good deal of grey in my hair as well but I kept it at bay with a dark rinse. All I had to do now was wash my hair frequently and not use the rinse. The first wash hurt like hell and set the cut bleeding but I'm a quick healer and I managed to stop the flow and avoid having to get it stitched.

I used the name Kelly at the hotel and kept pretty much out of sight. I cleaned the blood from the linen jacket but I didn't wear it. In a secondhand store I bought a well-used Panama that provided shade and further disguise. Tennis shoes, a faded blue work shirt and a leather jerkin transformed me from an affluent Californian into an Americano, one of many hanging around Tijuana for reasons best not looked into. The next step was to acquire identification I could use at the post office to collect my money. Not hard in a border town where document-forging is always a thriving concern. By judicious enquiry in the right places, by which I mean certain *cantinas* rather than the American Express office, I located the right man. For twenty-five dollars he doctored my Californian driver's licence so that Richard K. Browning of Sherman Oaks became Richard Kelly of San Francisco.

After four days I changed hotels, moving to Coahuila Street where every second building is a brothel, and carrying my few belongings in a canvas holdall. When I looked in the fly-spotted mirror the face I saw was unrecognisable as the one that had crossed the border. Paler, thinner and older, much older, with grey whiskers and white above the temples. Stoop the shoulders a little, and the prime-of-life tennis and riding coach changed into someone with many more years on the clock — a bullfight buff, a racetrack addict, maybe even a cut-price Ernest Hemingway.

I fronted up to the post office a little after siesta when everyone is still waking up and things are a bit slip-shod. Still, I looked it all over very carefully before making my move. The street sellers looked like street sellers, the clerks looked like clerks and the bums looked like bums. There was no one hiding behind a newspaper, no shiny shoes under frayed denims, no tilted forward sombreros with peep holes in the brim. I marched up to the counter and printed my name on the slip provided. The clerk reached back into the K pigeonhole and thumbed through the letters, selecting one that was much fatter than I'd expected.

'Identification, Senor.'

I handed over the licence and he barely glanced at it before flicking the letter across. I signed for it with a flourish and strolled away. If anyone had been on to me, now was the time to strike. The hair on the back of my neck bristled as I crossed the polished floor towards the doors. So far, so good. A tall, slim woman dressed in a white sharkskin suit was mounting the steps and I gallantly held the door open for her.

'Thank you.'

'You're welcome.'

She must have been close to six feet tall in her high heels. Her hair was a glossy black falling to her shoulders, and her impassive face was pale and perfect in every feature. Although the afternoon was still very hot, there wasn't a drop of perspiration on her face. Her walk was a sexual act. I goggled, hanging on to the door, quite forgetting that I was supposed to be alert for danger. Nothing happened. It was as if people had stopped breathing. Every male eye in the place was on her as she strode across to the counter. At that moment, I doubt that J. Edgar Hoover himself could have kept his mind on the job. I stumbled out of the building and down the steps into the street, clutching the envelope and needing a drink. I've talked to other men about this phenomenon and most agree that, at a few times in their lives, they've seen women that have made them tremble with desire and fear — for me, this was one of those occasions.

I returned to my senses after wandering along the streets for several minutes. I found a bar, ordered a beer and sat down to open my envelope. Louise had sent five hundred bucks which was a little disappointing but not too bad. Her letter was brief and to the point. She'd do what we agreed on the phone and wait for my call. She loved me and missed me. The bulk of the envelope was due to several newspaper clippings she'd enclosed. I didn't keep them because a sure way to blow a false identity is to carry around things about the person you're pretending not to be. But I memorised the cutting from the *San Fernando Post*.

The headline read, FBI IN RAID ON DRAMA COLLEGE, and the article went on to describe in the most vague, general and ultimately inaccurate terms what the reporter thought had happened. His problem was that he didn't know and no-one was going to tell him. He had me down as 'English born Richard Browning', very offensive to an Australian of Irish convict descent, but as things stood, the more confusion generated about me the better. The list of my film credits was a dog's breakfast of half-truths and outright lies. The story didn't allege that I'd been involved in any wrong-doing but the implication was clear. I could see Louise's point though, the whole thing had a racy air that smacked more of mystery and adventure than criminality. A small, blurry photograph of yours truly was a comfort — no one could possibly have identified me from it. There was a great picture of Louise in tennis gear putting all she had into a forehand drive. It was a beautiful thing to see, Louise's forehand, and the photograph made me yearn for her.

I sipped my beer and considered my options. I could stay put and hope that Louise's mouthpiece could smooth the way for me to go back to the States. One thing against this idea was that in all my dealings with them I'd never known a lawyer to do anything quickly, unless it was to present his bill. Another was that if the mob decided I needed some education, Tijuana was the place they'd begin looking. I could take a holiday in Mexico for a while, improve my Spanish and become an expert on tequila. Somehow, that didn't appeal to me. I just knew I'd get into trouble.

I reached into my pocket for some money to pay for the beer and along with the change and small bills came the drink coaster with James Dean's number scribbled on it. I'd completely forgotten about it and it was a wonder I still had it. I suppose I'd been careful about what I threw away. The numbers were faded from several days rubbing up against other things but still readable. Louise had said he wanted to talk to me and I couldn't think of a single other person in that category who wouldn't want to do a bit more than talk, like hit or shoot. *Why not*? I found a phone and rang the number.

'Yeah?'

'Is that James Dean?'

'Depends on who wants to know.'

'This is Dick Browning.'

The surly, up-you tone disappeared. 'Hey, Dick. That really you? Where're you ringin' from?'

'I'm in Mexico.'

"Mexico! Hey, wild!'

'Louise said you wanted to talk to me. If it's about the key to your motorbike, I took it because I thought you were too drunk to drive. I think I've still got it. I'll mail it to you.'

There was a slight pause while he digested that. Stars don't like to reminded of their mortality, although the smarter ones realise that it's good for them for it to happen once in a while. Dean was definitely in that category.

'That's ok,' he said. 'Guess you were right. I don't remember much about what happened after the Feds arrived. Reckon I had a few more drinks. Anyway, I got a spare key. But hey, that was a wild show you turned on. What's the story?'

'It's a long one and I can't really give it to you on the phone. I've got to lie low for a while, you understand.'

'Sure, but look, the job offer I made you holds good. In fact, it holds good in spades.'

'What job offer?'

'You don't remember? Shit, man, I want you around when we're on location in this shit-eatin' town in Texas. I can fix it so's you'll be on the payroll — personal assistant, adviser, somethin' like that. What d'you say?'

I could see some advantages — camouflage, influential associates, income. On the other hand I knew from experience that one definition of hell is being at the beck and call of a movie star and movie-obsessed people. But it was the best thing on offer. 'Where is this place?'

'Little town called Marfa in the middle of Texas. Goin' to be damn hot. They tell me it's near El Paso, if that means anything to you. So, you interested?'

'Yes, sure, Jimmy, I'm interested. When're you planning to be there?'

I heard the click of his lighter and that deep sucking sound he made on a cigarette. 'Flying out day after tomorrow. Going by way of Phoenix and someplace else. You get there and we'll have a ball, man.'

'Ok,' I said, 'I'll be there. Thanks, Jimmy. But there's one thing — I'll be Dick Kelly, not Browning. Understand?'

The giggle. 'I understand. And say, Dick, how about you bring up a pound or two of that good Mexican weed, huh?'

The operator cut in. I didn't have any more coins and the line went dead. I hung up and my first impulse was to forget the whole thing. Dean was an erratic character, just as likely to tell me to go to hell if I turned up, especially without any marijuana, and I had no intention of going into the drug smuggling business. Against that, I'd be back in the States, able to contact Louise and monitor how things were going on the legal front. It was still the best deal on the table.

I walked to the railway station and made a study of the routes and schedules. I had two choices: cross the border and travel by rail through California, Arizona and New Mexico into Texas or stay in Mexico and travel by bus to some point along the border. I felt I wasn't quite ready for the USA, so I bought a ticket to Mexicali where I could cross at Calexico. It was going to mean some boring waiting and some sweaty discomfort, but a lifetime of moving around, mostly under duress of one kind or another, had taught me that it's not the journey that counts, it's arriving in one piece.

Back at the hotel I noticed the difference in the desk clerk's manner at once. Where previously he had been slovenly and careless, barely noticing who came and went, now he was alert and a trifle too quick to hand me my key. I didn't say anything but my nerves were jangling as I went up the first flight of stairs. My room was on the second floor and I ran along the corridor on the floor below to the bathroom, climbed through the window and dropped into the alley. From the first time I ran out on a hotel bill in Sydney in 1916[23] I've made a habit of surveying the entrances and exits. It sometimes seems to me that I've gone out through windows and fire escapes more often than doors and front steps.

I ran down the alley, emerged into the street that ran parallel to Coahuila, walked a block and took up a position behind a stand of scruffy palm trees in a patchy garden opposite the hotel. I wanted to see which species of enemy was on my trail. After a few minutes two men emerged. They weren't the two who'd escorted

Luciano, Stompanato and me to the border, but they might just as well have been. Good suits, if a little warm for the day, clean shoes, fresh haircuts — polished gorillas. They conferred for a few minutes on the pavement, letting the swirl of Mexican humanity move around them as if it wasn't there. They were, as the sports players say nowadays, focussed.

One of them leaned into the Ford tourer that was parked at the kerb and spoke briefly to someone inside. The door opened and the brunette in the white suit stepped out. She crossed the street, seeming to glide through the traffic, took a seat under an umbrella at a pavement cafe not far from where I was hiding and lit a cigarette. One of the gorillas went back into the hotel and the other walked down a side street, headed for the rear of the building. They were going to have a lengthy and fruitless wait. I took a long look at the woman in the white suit. With the survival instinct working against every other one, I fervently hoped that I'd never see her again. I stepped back into the shadows and faded away in the direction of the bus station.

CHAPTER TWELVE

MEXICAN bus drivers are a special breed, which is not surprising, I suppose, because Mexican roads are unlike roads anywhere else in my experience. The bus was about half full when we pulled out of the depot in the mid-afternoon and I was reasonably comfortable with a three-person seat behind the driver to myself. An hour later, having made several stops around the city and in the outlying districts, it was crammed to the gills. And not all the passengers were humans; there were squawking chickens tied up by the legs, snakes in a basket and a live goat. The central aisle and the luggage racks were filled with bundles and packages and boxes and there was at least as much cargo loaded on the top of the bus as inside. A few kids sat up on the roof as well.

I was now sharing my seat with a fat woman and a fat girl who ate constantly — cold tortillas, bananas, sticky sugar cakes and hard candy. Every time the bus went around a sharp bend I was thrown against the woman and felt myself cannon off her soft, mushy flesh like a pool ball. She didn't speak to me or the kid, she was too busy eating. For the first ten or fifteen miles the ride was bedlam, with the passengers shouting and the chooks cackling and the driver keeping up a running stream of chatter with his assistant who squatted on the steps. The door didn't quite close and dust entered through the gap, swished around and seemed to settle in my throat. Once we'd got beyond the city the road became a corrugated dirt track with six inch potholes and randomly distributed rocks the size of footballs.

After an hour or so the racket settled down to a steady, low-pitched hum made up of noise from the bus's engine and chassis, the snoring of a lot of the passengers and the steady chomping of my neighbour's jaws. Most of the men smoked and I did too, to pass the time, and the interior of the bus was cloudy with the dust and smoke. The day was cooling fast, but the temperature inside was going up with the press of bodies. With that went an increase in the smells of humanity and livestock. Wealthy Mexicans travel by car or rail. Poorer people travel by bus and poor Mexicans, like poor people everywhere, don't wash much. Also beans make up a good part of the diet of working Mexicans, and everyone knows what that means. After three hours I'd have given a lot for one of the heavy, awkward gas masks they'd issued us with in the trenches in France in 1918.

At a market stall near the depot I'd bought a raffia basket and a few supplies — some dried fruit, fried bean cakes, bread, a couple of handsful of nuts wrapped in newspaper spills, cigarettes and a bottle of tequila. All I had was what I carried and stood up in and not a single weapon. Although I had almost six hundred dollars in my shirt pocket, probably enough to buy the bus, I looked as if I'd have had trouble raising ten. That was the way I wanted it. Several of my fellow passengers looked as if they'd disembowel their mothers for fifty bucks, let alone six hundred.

A hundred miles isn't far in a good car on a good road, but it felt like five times the distance in that bus on the narrow, winding road. The going never got so bad that the bus had to back up the way I've seen them do in some parts of the country, but there were plenty of times when we stopped to allow other vehicles to edge past and for herds of goats and mobs of sheep. People were set down and others taken on at places that looked like nothing more than a bend in the road. I waited until the sun was almost down behind the blue hills in the west before uncorking the tequila and taking a few quiet sips. The firewater washed away the dust and raised my spirits. I ate some bread and fruit, watched by the fat woman out of the corner of her eye.

My Spanish had picked up considerably since I'd been south of the border and I had no difficulty understanding her when she stopped chewing long enough to speak.

'Give me some tequila, gringo.'

'No,' I said. 'It would make you fat and it would be a pity to spoil your wonderful figure.'

She hooted with laughter and repeated the exchange to the people sitting behind us. They broke up too and passed it on. Sometimes it's easy to get a laugh. They spoke much too quickly for me to understand and I had a feeling I might have used the wrong word. Maybe I'd made her some kind of proposition. Eventually she and her gluttonous brat fell asleep. My money was securely buttoned into my shirt pocket. I took another few sips, folded my arms across my chest and tilted my hat forward. The road kept climbing and winding and didn't get any less rough, but I had a warm soft cushion beside me and after the day I'd had no power on earth could have kept me awake.

It was dark when we chugged into Mexicali, no time to go crossing the border unless you were a wetback hoping to earn fifty cents a day on a truck farm.[24] I checked into the cheapest hotel I could find that would provide me with a private bath. I bought soap and toothpaste and a toothbrush at an all-night drugstore down the street as well as a day-old issue of the Calexico paper, the *Border Post*. I soaked in the bath for over an hour, reading the paper, sipping tequila and eating nuts. The room also boasted a radio and a telephone, putting it quite a few notches up on the place I'd skipped out of at Tijuana. After the bath I listened to the news on a California station.

It was very unusual to hear a British accent on American radio and I pricked up my ears when I heard the tones of Oxbridge intermixed with the static. It was Roger Bannister who'd broken the four minute mile a few days earlier in a time trial specially arranged to do

PETER CORRIS

the job with pacers and other advantages. Never seemed quite the fair
way to go about it to me, but it was a terrific run.[25] It's a remarkable
fact, but I remember two other things about listening to the radio
that night — it was the first time I ever heard the word Vietnam
mentioned. The Vietnamese communists had beaten the French
army in a battle at a place called Dien Bien Phu. And right after the
news the station played a record by Bill Haley and the Comets called
'Rock around the Clock'. It sounded to me as if the drummer and
saxophonist and guitarists were beating each other around the head
with their instruments. Rock 'n' Roll and Vietnam and I forgot about
them instantly. It took only a few bars of Doris Day, more my sort of
thing, to wipe that noise from my mind completely.[26]

Relaxed and refreshed with my still wet body cooling nicely
under the ceiling fan, I rang Louise.

'Sherman House, Louise Browning speaking.'

The married name had never tripped off Louise's tongue easily
in the past. Now it sounded as if she'd been using it for years.

'Louise, this is Dick.'

'Dick, my god. I've been wondering when you'd call. Is everything all right? Where are you? You're not in gaol? They haven't
got you?'

I started to sweat and the room felt stuffy. 'What d'you mean,
got me? Of course I'm not in gaol. I'm still in Mexico.'

'Thank god. Dick, those FBI men have been very persistent.
They've been around asking questions, turning the place upside
down. Threatening me, almost. Quite different from the way they
were before.'

I poured a generous shot of tequila and lit a cigarette. 'Different?'

'Yes. Much more... aggressive. They really want to catch you
but... but... '

She sounded very distressed and I tried to keep my voice calm.
'But what, Louise? Take it easy, honey. I'm safe. Nothing's changed.
Tell me what's going on.'

'Mr Silkstein says the FBI didn't seem to be trying too hard to catch the gangster but they seem to be trying bloody hard to catch *you*. He wouldn't say anything more, but I think I know what he means. Are you some kind of undercover agent, Dick? I know so little about you, really. Are you working for the FBI? Or *were* you? I'm so confused, I don't know what to think.'

She was confused, what about me? I've been a lot of things in my time — wine salesman, actor, soldier, aviator, private eye, but I've never been a policeman, unless you count a brief spell in the Mounties, and that was really just a case of mistaken identity.[27] And as for being an undercover agent, the idea was ridiculous — way too dangerous a game for Dick. I was dumbfounded, couldn't think of anything to say, and just automatically hung up the phone. I took a deep drag on my cigarette and drank some tequila while my head filled with nightmare visions of mobsters and cops and G-men, all gunning for me.

One thing Bobby Silk had said rang true. It was difficult to believe that the authorities had tried really hard to stop Luciano. Why hadn't they posted men at the other exits from Sherman House? Why hadn't they radioed ahead to San Diego or other points south? There had been rumours that Luciano had done a deal with the Feds that had got him his parole and deportation. Was the deal still in operation and did someone in Washington not want yours truly floating around talking about how easily he skipped the country with Charley Lucky? I was willing to take any kind of oath of silence they liked, but that wouldn't satisfy anyone.

About then I realised that I'd hung up on my wife without offering her any kind of explanation or comfort. What else could she think but that I *was* some kind of cloak and dagger merchant? The ease and confidence I'd been feeling completely vanished. I felt that every man's hand was turned against me. Here I was, a completely innocent American citizen, a tax-paying veteran, hiding out in a two-bit hotel in a foreign country. I needed money, a lawyer, a friend and constitutional rights and the only place I had a hope of getting them was about a mile away in the United States of America.

CHAPTER THIRTEEN

THERE was no song in my heart when I inspected the border crossing the next day. It looked simple enough — a bridge over the river, a walkway beside it, plenty of coming and going of motor traffic. A few minutes' study was sufficient to reveal my problem. Not a single gringo crossed into the US on foot. They were all in cars, mostly with Californian plates, but a scattering of Texan and Arizonan. The guards waved them through with scarcely a look, but if I was to stroll along that walkway with my raffia bag in my hand I'd stand out like a camel in a horserace. The Mexicans who were crossing on foot — presumably to day jobs in Calexico — were either known to the guards or showed some kind of pass. No hope of buying a sombrero and passing myself off as a Mex.

I mooched back towards the town, discouraged but not defeated. If I could hitch a ride with some other Americans I'd be fine. Failing that I'd have to dip into my slender capital and buy a car. I gave the second idea up at once. There were several used-car dealers in Mexicali, but not one of them had a vehicle with US plates. I enquired about this at one place and the proprietor misunderstood me.

'Yes, Senor? You have some American plates for sale? I can get you top price. Which state? California, yes?'

'No, I'm asking about *cars* with American plates. You don't have any for sale?'

He burst out laughing. 'Senor, you are joking. For a set of American plates I would trade you any three cars on this lot. No, any four cars!'

The cars were cheap, but I got the idea. My next move was to hang around a few of the hotels in the hope of scrounging a lift. Again, no luck. Most of the American car drivers were either family men with full loads or heading further into Mexico. The few possibles, some college kids who'd crossed the border for purposes better not dwelt on, and a pair of female anthropologists who'd been working in a village to the south, were much too wary to offer their services to a seedy-looking individual like me. I took a walk along the river, vaguely thinking that I might cross it at some point downstream. Along that stretch the Rio Grande is nothing like the way it appears in the Westerns when the outlaws gallop across it and the posse turns back except for Gregory Peck.[28] Here the river wasn't wide, nor deep or fast moving, but it had fifty yards of treacherous-looking muddy bank on either side. On the American side the bank was steep and rugged. There was no way to get through those two mud flats, the water and the wilderness and still look like a solid citizen.

I wandered on a bit but nothing changed. I was now a mile or so out of town and I came to an outdoor market beside the road where villagers were selling their produce. Behind the market a circus had set up. Not much of a circus; just a big tent and a few countrified sideshow attractions like horse-shoe-throwing, a coconut shy and a clay pigeon shoot. The animals, an elderly lion, a quiet tiger and a couple of bored bears, were asleep in their cages. I took a look inside the tent where a not-very-high wire was set up over the sawdust with a couple of trapezes and a slightly sagging and much-mended safety net. The whole show evidently could be folded up and put inside a big Dodge truck that hauled the animal cages and a couple of trailers attached to a Ford pickup. I heard a few shots and went over to the clay-pigeon shoot where the deal was that if you could outshoot the celebrated marksman, Hartley Grattan, you could win yourself a thousand pesos. Cost you a hundred to try. Grattan was a Frank Butler[29] type, with the sideburns, Stetson, fringed buckskin jacket and all.

I watched him take a few practice shots and wasn't wildly impressed. He seemed to me to swing a trifle slow and to take the target a bit below the desirable point — at the top of its arc. Still, he only missed once in three shots. When he broke the shotgun to shake out the shells I thought his hand trembled just a fraction. The guy working the target firer lined up several discs and straightened up, stretching his back. He was about sixty years old with a folded-in face and hooded dark eyes that had seen it all. He took out a tobacco pouch and stuffed a pipe. Grattan just stood staring out over the firing range with slightly bloodshot eyes.

'Have a shot, mister?' The pipe was alight and he pointed the stem at a rack of three shotguns.

'Maybe.' I inspected the guns. Two had bent barrels and the third, although straight, had a cracked stock and bad balance. I shook my head. 'Not with this junk. Couldn't hit a barn door with them at twenty feet. How about I use his gun and he uses one of these?'

The pipe-smoker looked me over carefully before sticking out his hand. 'I'm Barney Slocum and this is my circus. You look like a sporting gentleman. Things are slow. You interested in a sporting wager?'

I shook his hand and pointed at the hand-painted sign. 'It says a hundred a shot.'

'That's for the rubes. I can tell from the way you handled them guns that you know shooting. Hartley here's a mite bored. A proper bet might get his spirits up some.'

My spirits could have used some raising too but I wasn't looking to be conned and I passed another uncomplimentary remark about the shotguns. Slocum brushed this aside and told Grattan to go fetch his spare gun. The shooter wandered off without commenting.

'What's the matter with him?' I asked. 'Is he a deaf mute or something?'

Slocum took off his greasy fedora and scratched at a balding head. 'He's a moody guy. I've known him go weeks without talking. Then he drinks some and you can't shut him up. Strange man, but he sure can shoot. Been with me a year or more and I've never seen him beat.'

It was hot and dusty and we were in a two-bit circus outside a crummy Mexican border town. Slocum must have known what I was thinking because he waved everything we could see away with a majestic flick of the hand. 'I'm not talking about this. I'm talking about cities — 'Frisco, Los Angeles, Mexico City — real shooters in some of them places.'

Before I could ask Slocum what he was doing slumming in Mexicali, Grattan came back carrying a Purdey shotgun that looked like a slightly older version of the one he'd been shooting. He handed it to me and I checked it over. It was a fine weapon, well-maintained, and it had a good, comfortable feel.

'Hartley won the Purdey he uses now in a big competition in New York,' Slocum said. 'And how much cash money, Hartley?'

'Thousand dollars.'

A few people had wandered up, apparently curious about the appearance of another gun and at the serious conversation the gringos were having. I swung and sighted with the Purdey a few times and felt confident I could shoot pretty well with it. As long as your eyes hold out, shooting ability is something you never lose, and I still had the eyesight of a young man. I took off my sunglasses, blinked a few times and let my eyes adjust to the bright light.

'What've you got in mind, Mr Slocum?'

'Straight two-man shoot. Toss for first gun. Ten shots. Twenty dollars a side. Winner take all.'

I took two tens from my roll, taking care not to let Slocum get a good look at it, and placed them in the box where he was keeping the expended shells. Then I loaded the shotgun from a box of Remingtons. There was another box containing home-loaded shells. They're fine if the loader knows what he's doing, but I preferred to trust the factory product.

'Two sighting shots,' I said.

Slocum nodded and put a twenty in the box. The Mexicans gathered around were displaying real interest now. Twenty dollars US was a lot of money. Slocum crouched by the target-firer with his pipe in his mouth.

I took my stance, breathed in and out a few times. 'Pull!'

The projectile soared, I sighted, fired and missed.

'Pull!'

I got the second one at exactly the right point, just before it began to drop, when there is an illusion that it's stationary. We tossed a coin. Grattan won and shot first. We shot five each. I missed once and so did Grattan. Draw. Same money up and we shot again with me taking first shot. Five hits apiece. Another draw. After another round we were still tied. By now the crowd had grown to fifty or more, all talking excitedly and making side bets of their own. Grattan and I tossed again to see who would shoot first and the quarter stood on its end.

'This could go on forever,' Slocum said. He flipped the coin again and I won. The stakes were now up to a hundred bucks, which was more than those Mexicans would have seen in a year. And it was more than I wanted to lose.

Grattan took off his jacket and wiped sweat from the band of his Stetson. He mopped his face with a handkerchief and flapped his arms to free his shirt which was sticking to his ribs and back. I was sweating too, but it's never a good idea to let an opponent see your discomfort. I made sure there was no sweat in my eyes or on my hands and didn't worry about the rest of me. I kept a close watch on

Slocum to make sure he didn't pull a swiftie with the shotgun shells or the targets but he seemed to be playing it straight. He kept up a stream of talk with the Mexicans in fluent Spanish. I only caught a snatch or two, but I gathered that opinion was about evenly divided on which of us would win.

After four shots we were still locked together. My shoulder was aching from the recoil of the shotgun. The Mexicans were now cheering each shot.

'Pull!' The disc soared and I saw it as if it was the size of a dinner plate. I drew on it and fired and the thing shattered into a grey cloud. The crowd whooped and hollered and I could hear the clinking of coins.

Grattan looked relaxed, called for his target, drew on it and missed. The crowd cheered wildly as I picked up the money from the box. Slocum was stunned. Grattan simply stood and stared out to a point where the disc had landed. His eyes swivelled, following its path. He shook his head slowly, broke his gun and took out the shells. He flipped them into the box where the money had been and reloaded.

'You're a damned fine shot, sir,' he said in a southern drawl. 'Might I know your name?'

'Dick B...Kelly. It could have gone either way.' I unloaded the gun and handed it to him.

Suddenly there was a great clamour from the Mexicans and Slocum started shouting in Spanish and waving his hands around. Grattan walked away carrying both shotguns. If ever I saw a man in search of a drink it was him. Then I heard Slocum laughing and the sound of guns being loaded.

'What's happening?' I asked.

Two Mexicans were lining up on the shooting mats and another was crouched by the target firer. 'Would you believe it?' Slocum chortled. 'They want to shoot against each other. Willing to pay five hundred pesos a round and the guy putting out the targets is paying two hundred and fifty. I'm well up on this deal, and lookit them others. They all want to get into the act. Mister, you just jumped my business up a couple hundred per cent.'

I stood with Slocum and we watched the Mexicans shoot it out. None of them was much good but they all had a hell of a lot of fun and the betting was fast and furious. The action only stopped when Slocum ran out of targets. He examined the bundle of battered, greasy notes and the heaps of coins. 'Ought to give you a cut by rights.'

'Don't worry about it,' I said. 'I came out ahead. You're right about Grattan. He's a hell of a good shot, just let that last one get a little slow. I have the feeling he's not quite at his best.'

Slocum nodded. 'Man's got problems. Liquor and women. Was there ever a worse combination?'

'Or a better one.'

He laughed. 'Sure, that's right. Yeah. Well, a woman took old Hartley for everything he had and that's why he joined up with me. Something of a drop in class for him I admit.'

'What're you doing down here, if you don't mind me asking? Pickings must be pretty lean.'

'Sure are. Well, just for a change of scene, you know? And Hartley, he wanted to get himself a Mexican divorce. Got it all right, but I reckon he's still pining for the same woman.'

'Good to meet you, Mr Slocum. I enjoyed myself.' I put out my hand but he ignored it, making a great play of stuffing his pipe and getting it lit.

'Now look here, Dick, I can't just let you walk away like this. You've put me on to a money-spinner. You don't look as if you've got too much money to keep that century company. What say you join up with me? We put on a match between you and Hartley, just like now, and then every other guy in the audience fancies himself a sharp-shooter. I reckon there's money to be made, and you'd get your share.'

My shoulder was aching and I knew I'd been lucky to beat Hartley. Also I didn't fancy dragging myself around Mexico in a circus. I knew how circus people lived, having done a stint of it myself way back.[30] It's all third-rate hotels, bad food and cheap liquor. I lit a cigarette and went through the motions of appearing to consider the proposition, but ended by shaking my head.

'No thanks, Mr Slocum. I appreciate the offer but I've got business back in the States in a few weeks. I've had enough of Mexico.'

'Who said anything about staying in Meh-hi-co? We're crossing the border tomorrow and heading for El Paso.'

Browning's luck, and skill, of course.

CHAPTER FOURTEEN

CROSSING the border was a breeze. I rode in the truck with Slocum at the wheel and the border guards looked more closely at the animals than the humans. The circus staff consisted of Grattan, Jack and Elsie Turnbull who acted as high-wire and trapeze performers as well as manning the horse-shoe ring and coconut shy, Joe Campesi who was a clown and animal trainer both and a half-Navaho roustabout named Ben who could fill in for just about anyone else at a pinch. It was a shoe-string affair, operating with modest expectations on low turn-over and low overhead. Slocum was proprietor, manager, cook, paymaster and money-lender. He was a decent man who treated the company right, keeping Grattan off the liquor and Ben away from Elsie.

I stayed with Slocum's circus for almost three weeks, playing small towns along the border and slowly relaxing into a casual way of life after my time of stress. Sometimes I beat Grattan in the shoots and sometimes he beat me. He was a better shot in fact, but his moodiness and occasional late-night bottle sessions dropped him back a notch into my class. As Slocum had expected, the format worked as well in California, Arizona and Texas as it had in Mexico, maybe better. These westerners were used to guns of all kinds and stationary and moving targets, but only at ground level. They shattered thousands of bottles per year and blasted hundreds of jack rabbits and desert critters to kingdom come, but the fast-flying, easy-to-see-hard-to-hit clay targets were a novelty they couldn't resist.

Slocum adjusted his prices to the prosperity or otherwise of the crowd. He was a shrewd judge of marksman and there were some real sharp-shooters among the audience — ranch hands, coyote killers and men who had served in the Second World War and Korea. Slocum took to making bets himself on the contests and he won more often than he lost. He was as good as his word — paying me a base salary and giving me a small cut of the takings. He was a busy man, attending to all the other aspects of the circus operation as well as the shooting and I was amazed at his energy. It was hard to tell how old he was or how much of his stories to believe. He claimed to have played for the New York Yankees, to have swum in the 1928 Olympics and to have had a hand in training Jack Dempsey. He said that Dempsey had used plaster of Paris against Willard and he claimed that Sharkey went into the tank against Camera.[31] He was an entertaining man to listen to.

All in all, it wasn't such a bad life, although I quickly got tired of the routine of the shoot-outs and the sameness of the country towns. I hit Sydney when I was a teenager and I've been a city man all my life. For me, the city represents good health and comfort and the backwoods the reverse — mostly because of the number of times I've had to run and hide among the rocks and trees. I could have stood it for a few months at least and built a solid bankroll, but I was anxious about my future and missing Louise. Hollywood is no place to leave a pretty young wife if you want to hang on to her, and the more miles I travelled on back roads and the more times I ate Slocum's basic meal of beans and bacon, the more anxious I became to take up James Dean's offer.

I left the circus in El Paso with Slocum's thanks and best wishes, a nod from Grattan and no tears from anyone else. Circus folks are used to the passing parade. El Paso was hot and dry and looked more Spanish than American. I took a room in a good hotel and set about improving my appearance. A haircut and beard trim got rid of the Wild West look that had been useful to Slocum, and I spent some money on clothes — lightweight casuals, a seersucker suit, a quality denim outfit and some tooled leather riding boots with chased silver buckles. I threw away the dirty Panama and the sweat-stained cowboy hat Grattan had lent me along with his second-best Purdey and invested in a brand new Stetson with a woven leather band. When I boarded the train for Marfa I looked like a prosperous cattleman and I did what I'd promised myself all those miles in that rattletrap Dodge truck — I travelled first class.

Before getting on the train in El Paso, I did a very unusual thing for me — I bought a book. It was Edna Ferber's best-seller *Giant*, and I figured I ought to know a bit more of what it was about. Louise had given me the gist of course, but that was all from the woman's point of view. Who had fallen in love with who and how everybody had *felt* about things. I wanted to know what *happened*. I read some of the book on the train and I was pretty impressed by the opening when all the rich assholes in Texas fly to the birthday party of the richest and biggest asshole of all — Jett Rink. I could well see that Jimmy Dean would have a lot of fun playing that part.

I'm no great reader, never have been, but there was something about reading the book, with its descriptions of the plains and the sky and the winds as the train rolled across the exact same kind of landscape, that held me for an hour or so. Maybe I'll take up reading some day, although I doubt it. I have to admit that expressions like a 'Jovian quadrille' leave me totally in the dark.[32] I skimmed the book and didn't finish it, but I read enough to see that there was a movie in it. Good scenes of cattle driving, a few convenient deaths and some sob stuff about the poor Mexicans. I'd have been a bit worried if I'd been Rock Hudson's agent. For my money the standout scene in the book was when Jett Rink strikes oil. I could imagine Dean playing that for all it was worth and stealing the picture. I'd only seen Hudson in a few forgettable things like *Has Anybody seen my Gal?* and *The Lawless Breed*. I couldn't see him stealing a scene from James Dean or even holding his own, and I hadn't even seen Dean *act!*

What should have been a pleasant eight-hour trip ending in the early evening turned into a nineteen-hour misery. First, there was a signals failure that held us up for four hours, then there was a derailment where the main line met a spur and that cost another six hours. We had to try to get some sleep in our seats which is never easy and the food and drink on the train were inadequate to the demands of the tired, angry travellers. I was one of the tiredest and angriest and I made fairly heavy use of the bottle of Wild Turkey I'd had the foresight to bring with me. I played poker with a couple of drummers and lost, not soothing to my temper. I was bone weary, half-drunk and gritty-eyed when the train finally rolled into Marfa just before dawn.

The railway station itself was almost deserted but there were plenty of people nearby, all standing behind a rope and watching what was happening near a little double-track shunting line slightly off to one side. It was the sort of thing I'd seen hundreds of times — cameras, lights, people in position, actors ready to act and technicians ready to be technical. There was no doubt who was the boss — a stocky, thick-waisted man in baggy drill trousers, open-neck shirt and white Stetson. There were more cameras set up than you'd usually expect to see for a scene like this, but I was to discover that was George Stevens' signature. He shot everything from every angle you could think of and some you couldn't.

A train that looked to be in better working order than the one I'd travelled on was shunted slowly onto the line and a calaboose that had been standing by was attached.

Frantic activity beside the line then a shout of 'Quiet, please!' Stevens pulled off his heavy horn-rims and gestured for the cameras to roll. The train backed up and then pulled slowly into shot. It stopped. A handtruck with a coffin on it was rolled into place. The train pulled out and when the last carriage was gone the handtruck with the coffin was left there, silhouetted against the dawn sky. Impressive stuff — the return home of Angel Obregon, Mexican war hero, killed in Korea. Not a dry eye in the house.

As they began to set up for another take — Stevens wouldn't have shot a scene in just one take on principle — I wandered over in the direction of the gaping locals. It looked as if most of the townsfolk were there — babies, grandparents, teenagers, the rich and the poor. The making of the movie must have been the biggest thing ever to hit Marfa. As usual, there was a hell of a lot of standing around waiting for things to happen. The Marfans didn't seem to mind. Some of them had coffee in thermoses and sandwiches and looked ready to make a real picnic of it.

The sky was clear and there was no wind. The sun wasn't yet up and the air was warming fast. A real Texas summer day was brewing and it was lucky for the technicians making adjustments to the flag-draped handcart and supervising the positioning of the train that the scene was being shot so early. Later on, their jobs would be hot ones. Stevens, puffing on a pipe, pointed, waved, barked orders. He looked like a man who knew what he wanted and wasn't interested in discussion. I couldn't help wondering how he'd get on with James Dean. The Marfa folk were laughing and chattering, swilling coffee and smoking, but they all fell dead silent when the command was given.

They shot the scene again. I couldn't see any difference from the first take and neither could some of the spectators. A few broke away and headed off towards their daily business. I'd seen towns besotted by movie-making before. The fascination usually lasts a couple of days before the people find out that it's one of the most boring activities in the world to watch. Stevens was being smart. If the director tries to keep the locals away, shrouds the whole thing in mystery, the fascination lasts longer. The more people hanging around a set the greater the chance of an interruption or a mistake. The best way to get rid of the gawkers is to give them as much of a look as they want right at the start.

PETER CORRIS

Movie directors may think of themselves as gods and behave like them but they can't stop the sun from coming up at its own pace. Stevens wanted another take and everyone was stepping on the gas to get the shot before the light was wrong. They got it, and the handcart carrying the coffin, which had been treated as if it was made of glass, was unceremoniously rolled away. The crowd started to disperse.

'Bullshit, pure bullshit.'

My recollection is that I smelt him before I saw or heard him, but maybe all three happened at once. He'd been hanging around on the edge of the crowd. He was wearing a plaid car coat with the fleecy collar turned up hiding most of his face. Dark glasses and a forward-tilted hat completed the disguise. James Dean, muttering to himself and smelling of sweat, stale tobacco and wine.

'It wasn't so bad,' I said. 'Anyway, it's in the book.'

'Fuck the book. Who're you?'

'It's Dick Browning, Jimmy.'

He took off his glasses and squinted at me. I think that was the first time I realised how short-sighted he was. 'I knew that,' he said.

CHAPTER FIFTEEN

MARFA was a desert town, very hot and dry, especially that year when the region was experiencing a drought. Water was in short supply. The air was supposed to be healthy for its cleanness but I never noticed any improvement in my health in the time I was there. The movie people had had a big impact on the place, soaking up most of the available hotel space and renting a number of houses for the leading players. Some members of the company were billeted on local families and cash was flowing into the economy of the town on a grand scale. On the other hand, the townsfolk had to put up with various inconveniences like an extra load on the already stretched water supply, interruptions to the town traffic and some eccentric behaviour, so I guess the Marfans thought it was fair to try to get as much out of the event as they could.

Dean was sharing a house with Rock Hudson and Chill Wills and he drove me there in a red convertible, treating it with considerable contempt, stubbing his cigarettes out on the dashboard because the ashtrays were overflowing.

'No motor cycle,' I said.

'Banned,' he said moodily. 'Like just about every goddamn thing. But hey, Dick, I'm real glad you turned up. This picture is a bitch to work on.'

'Aren't they all.'

'I guess so, but this is special. Here's the house. Just moved in t'other day. Liz Taylor's across the street.'

The house was a large, comfortable ranch-style building, like a prosperous smalltown doctor or lawyer might own. Dean left the car parked at the beginning of the driveway where it would be sure to obstruct his fellow tenants and clomped across the grass to the porch. He was wearing denims and cowboy boots, both items of clothing completely filthy. He shucked off his coat to reveal a blue work shirt, encrusted with sweat and grime, and a sleeveless denim jacket.

'Be hot as a whore's asshole in an hour,' he said, 'an' I've gotta do my first scene with Liz. Mean to tell you, man, I'm nervous.'

I followed him into the house and put my valise in the hall. I didn't figure to be staying in the stars' digs. Dean stomped through to the kitchen, humming to himself and snapping his fingers.

'Gotta woman here cooks for us. I think Chill's bangin' her, but she might be around some place. You want a li'l breakfast?'

He was working hard on his Texas accent and doing pretty well. I said that there'd been no food to speak of on the train and that some eggs and coffee would go down well.

'Betty!' he yelled. 'Betty, you there?' There was no response and he shook his head. 'Slut. No breakfast. Guess I can fix some coffee.'

He was looking thin and hollow-cheeked and his movements were listless. We went out to the kitchen which was dirty and untidy in that bachelor way. The table was littered with newspapers, magazines, glasses, cups and ashtrays. He made a mess of the coffee preparations, spilling the stuff and over-filling the pot. I took over and he sat on the kitchen table, staring down at his dirty boots and smoking. 'The thing is,' he said, 'this picture's weird. They didn't pay Edna Ferber anything much for her book. She's got big points in the movie. And George Stevens has got a lot of his own money in it. You know what that means.'

'Sure. Means it *has* to work or they're in the shit. Doesn't make it any easier.'

'Right. Plus Rock Hudson can't act, less'n he was cast as a fence post or something. Liz Taylor's not happy either.'

I poured coffee and got cream from the refrigerator. Jimmy waved that away and began spooning sugar into the cup. He must have put in four big spoonsful, all it could hold. Then he started stirring. He seemed more interested in stirring it than drinking it. I took cream, a bit of sugar and drank it as fast as I could.

'What's her problem?'

'Outfits for one thing. She says they're trying to make her look like a lesbian in drag — heavy shoes, lumpy stuff, and this is when she's supposed to be *young*! She says if they wanted an old dike they should've cast Dietrich.' He gave that crazy giggle and went on stirring.

'And how about you, Jimmy?'

He dropped his cigarette into the coffee and pushed the cup away. 'Ah'm gettin' bah. Shit, I haven't got a hell of a lot to do. Gotta make the most of it. Stevens, he's an old woman. Plays it sooo safe. He shoots about ten times what he needs and moans about it on account of it's his money. But that's not the real problem... '

He broke off to light another cigarette and I poured myself more coffee. He squinted at me through the smoke and rubbed at his eyes.

'What've *you* been doing since you drove that gangster out of town? On the run in Mexico, shit. That's really something. You got a gun, Dick?'

'No. What would...'

The telephone rang. He seemed to consider ignoring it but finally slid off the table and ambled out of the room, trailing smoke behind him. I heard him mumble a few words, then there was the sound of water running. He came back with his face washed and his hair slicked down, scrubbing away with a toothbrush. 'Gotta go do that fuckin' scene,' he said around the brush. 'Come with, Dick. You're on the payroll as of now.'

As what? I wanted to ask, but he'd picked up a copy of the script from the debris on the table and was heading fast towards the door. I followed, tired, still hungry and grubby, but not wanting to let go of the only person I knew in the whole state of Texas.

The scene they were shooting was the first encounter between Leslie and Jett, when she is overcome by the heat and Bick orders Jett to drive her back to the house. It was shot out on the prairie with the cattle standing around and once again there was a fair-sized crowd of townspeople in a roped-off area out of camera range. They'd driven to the shoot and maybe they were hoping to get a sneaky lookin; if so they were out of luck because George Stevens knew all about keeping yokels out of shot. Dean's hands were shaking as he took a last look at the script.

'Stick around,' he grunted at me before lighting a cigarette, dropping the script on the seat and mooching over to the make-up tent. I could see Rock Hudson and Mercedes McCambridge standing around under umbrellas talking to Stevens. For my money they all needed makeup and plenty of it. They were many shades paler than the Texans and I'm not talking about Mexicans or Indians. Elizabeth Taylor emerged from the tent and I have to say she looked pretty good. As out of place in that landscape as a bear on a beach of course, but that sort of thing has never worried Hollywood. She wore an olive-green riding outfit with a brown hat and tan boots. She had a sweet smile for everyone as she took up her spot near the jalopy Jett was to drive her away in.

I took a look at the script. James Dean was supposed to get out of the car and make a fumbling attempt at gallantly handing her in. Then he had to respond to Bick's instructions. You were supposed to see that he hated Bick and was already halfway in love with Leslie — not too hard to get across. I left the car and joined the people behind the rope, half hoping that some kind soul would offer me a sandwich. No one did.

'Isn't he cute?' a bobbysoxer in the crowd said as Dean sauntered into view and fell into consultation with Stevens. Stevens was waving and pointing. Jimmy, of course, was looking at his boots as if his lines were written on the toecaps.

'He's a bum is what he is,' a big, rawboned ranch-hand said. He spat a stream of tobacco juice not too far from the girl's tasselled loafers.

'Well, I think he's cute.'

'He's a candy-assed faggot.'

I left them to their dialogue and pushed through to the rope to get a better view of the shoot. Again, Stevens had cameras set up all over the place and I got the feeling that if he could've drawn lines on the ground for the actors to walk along he would have. He was still talking but Dean was now staring up into the pale blue sky.

Eventually it was action stations, but Jimmy kept backing away from his spot, shaking his head and puffing on a cigarette. It looked like a bad case of stage fright to me. Elizabeth Taylor knew how to handle herself. She stood very still and seemed to glow, perhaps not quite the right look if she was supposed to be sun-struck, but that was the director's problem. Suddenly, Dean detached himself and began to walk towards the roped section.

'He's comin' ovah heah!' a girl squealed.

About fifty yards away he stopped, unzipped his fly, pulled out his cock and pissed long and hard onto a small mesquite bush. The bush offered no concealment. When he finished he gave it a good shake, tucked it away and walked back to the set. No one in the crowd moved or spoke. Stevens called for quiet and signalled for action. Everyone, including Jimmy, went through their highly-paid motions. Even from the distance I was at, I could see that Dean was getting all he could from the scene, twitching a little as Hudson spoke his line, angling his body as he reached to open the car door so as to make the movement interesting in itself, ducking his head as he spoke. Standard stuff for a scene-stealer, but done with a lot of flair and, most dangerous for the other actors, perfectly in keeping with the Jett Rink character and difficult to criticise.

They did the bit in three or four takes and if Stevens was trying to tone Dean down it didn't work. He played the scene his way, even to the way he drove the car away with a series of lazy movements that *almost* took too long. Almost but not quite. The man was a master of timing at twenty-four years of age. Only after the filming finished did the people begin to talk about the pissing incident. It was something like a religious event. I actually heard one woman say that it hadn't happened, that he'd only pretended to piss. Someone else maintained that the urine was the colour of blood and that James Dean must be a very sick man. The tobacco-chewer opined that he should be bull-whipped and tarred-and-feathered. I was getting some idea of the power Dean exerted over people's imaginations and emotions.

The dust from the car's departure was still hanging in the hot air when I saw Dean wave me towards his convertible. I began to walk towards it when a young man I was to learn was an actor named Dennis Hopper came running up. He put his hand on Dean's shoulder and spun him around, almost tipping him off balance. Dean feinted a punch at his chin and gave him a lop-sided smile.

'I've seen you do some crazy things,' Hopper said, 'but what in hell was that all about?'

Dean adjusted his sunglasses. 'I was so nervous on account of Liz,' he said, 'that I just plain couldn't speak. I figured if I could take a piss in front of all those people I could do anything in front of a couple of goddamn cameras.'[33]

Hopper shook his head and walked away. Dean winked at me. 'Dennis Hopper. He was with me in *Rebel*. Nice guy, but he thought he was the greatest young actor in the world. Guess he's having another think.'

We got in the car and I was hoping we might go somewhere that served food but Jimmy didn't seem intent on going anyplace. The fact was, he loved cars, all kinds, stationary and moving. Sitting in a car was one of his favourite activities. He fished out a cigarette, got it lit and leaned back in the driver's seat. My stomach was growling and I was having trouble concentrating on what he was saying. He mumbled so badly it was possible to miss fifty per cent anyway. Mostly, it didn't matter. I caught the words hotel and assistant and I gathered that he'd arranged for me to stay at the house and to go on the payroll as his personal assistant.

'Doing what?' I said. 'You already know how to steal a scene from Elizabeth Taylor. What help could you possibly need?'

'Nothing like that. Not roping and riding. None of that shit. I need you as a personal bodyguard — we've been getting death threats.'

CHAPTER SIXTEEN

I took a careful look at him as he drove. He was elated after the successful shoot and pleased with his prank. I wondered if he'd been over-indulging any of the substances then popular among the Hollywood wild ones — benzedrine, marijuana etc. I'd heard that they could bring on persecution complexes and acute anxiety. I'd tried pot a few times but preferred bourbon. I hadn't noticed any increased anxiety but then, I'm fairly anxious most of the time. He was smoking as always, not taking the cigarette from his mouth, just sucking the smoke in and letting it leak away, almost as if he was eating it sloppily. Not pretty to watch. But he didn't seem any more twitchy than usual.

'Why I asked you about the gun,' he said. 'You know, Dick, the word was, with some people, you were kinda working *with* the Feds on that gangster thing. Any truth in that?'

Never confirm, never deny — that's someone's motto, can't quite remember whose. Anyway, there's a lot to be said for it and a man of mystery is a lot more interesting than a pane of glass. 'I can't say.'

'Uh huh. I don't suppose you brought me any grass, did you?'

I shook my head.

'Which leaves me still wondering. If you were a Fed and wanted to cause me trouble you had your chance right there.'

I was suddenly aware that he was driving much too fast for the state of the road and the amount of attention he was giving to driving. Up ahead was a cross road and I could see another car approaching it at speed on the left. It looked as if we'd reach the intersection at the same time.

I pointed. 'See him there?'

Dean nodded although I was fairly sure he hadn't seen the other car — a dusty pick-up, difficult to spot in that light against the dun background. 'I see him an' he'll see me.'

He slammed his foot down and roared through, missing the truck by a couple of feet. I felt my stomach lurch and was glad I hadn't had anything to eat.

'You don't have to worry about death threats,' I said shakily. 'You're going to kill yourself. Slow down or fucking well let me out!'

He giggled but he eased back on the throttle. 'I'm too good a driver. I've won races, man. Seriously, we're getting death threats from these crazy Mex-Texans. I need someone to watch my back. It's me they're after.'

'Why's that?'

'You read the book?'

'Some of it.'

'Some's enough. This Jett Rink character, he hates Mexicans. Says real bad things about 'em and in the end won't let them come to his party. There's some Mexican hotheads down here don't want the picture being made on account of that.'

I tried to recall details from the book which were already hazy just a few hours later. 'Doesn't Bick Benedict dislike Mexicans, too? He's against his wife getting the doctor for them and so on.'

Dean nodded. 'Employs 'em though, lets 'em in his house. Besides, Rock Hudson, he's protected. Got a man with him night and day, if you know what I mean.'

'How about Liz? Her character *likes* Mexicans. Wouldn't there be some folk down here taking a dim view of that. Sort of nigger-loving kind of thing?'[34]

'I don't know. I'm worried about my own ass.'

He was very honest in that way, James Dean. What they'd now call up-front. We'd reached the town and Dean was driving sedately, responding to my outburst and anxious to please — virtually the only time I'd seen him in this mode. He was serious and I was curious. Someone who played with a high horsepower motor cycle, who drove fast in sport car races and recklessly on the public highways the way he did, who was a boozer and pot-smoker, couldn't be all that concerned with his physical safety.

Being one myself and acutely attuned to the condition, I didn't get the feeling that James Dean was a physical...I won't say coward...was a physically cautious person.

'This movie's my big chance, Dick,' he said. '*Eden* didn't do much business and who knows how *Rebel* will be received — kids, cars, who knows? This is a great big fuckin' soap opera, but it gives me something to work with. I can be a star, man, and after that, just maybe I can be an actor. You know what I mean? I don't want some political nutcases fucking it up.'

I understood and I believed him — naked self-interest is always the most honest, uncomplicated and powerful of motives. I had to consider my own safety though.

'How did these death threats come — over the phone, through the mail, what?'

'Letters.'

That made me feel better. Letter-writers seldom *do* anything. The job sounded as if it would involve a lot of sitting around killing time, but it would give me a base from which to work my way back to LA. 'I'm in,' I said. 'What d'you want me to do?'

'Hang around and keep your eyes open. You'd better get hold of a gun. Every second son of a bitch in town's got one.'

'I'll need a vehicle.'

He thumped the wheel, making the car swerve and skid. He corrected the skid pretty competently and flicked his butt out over the bonnet. 'You can take this piece of junk. I'm sick of it. Think I'll get me a jeep from the motor pool.'

That was one he didn't manage to swing. No one in his right mind would have put James Dean in charge of a jeep.

I freshened up at the house while Jimmy looked over the script for his next scene. Betty, the housekeeper, reluctantly made me some toasted ham sandwiches and I drank coffee to keep myself awake. Betty was a middle-aged woman, rapidly running to fat, who very quickly had found out that film stars were not necessarily nice or tidy. I was just one more man for her to pick up after and she treated me accordingly. I delivered Jimmy to the next location and hung around while they filmed a short scene that looked wrong to me and it didn't make it into the movie. Then he was to be in conference with Stevens for an hour, so I had that time free.

Marfa was the seat of Presido county and I'd spent enough time in rural America to know that, if you're going to be carrying a gun and taking part in the peace-keeping business, you'd better first clear it with the county sheriff. Sheriff Howard 'Hud' Clayhorn's office was in an adobe building behind the courthouse, a block back from Main Street. I was nervous about venturing into an inner sanctum of the law, but I figured that any pictures of me on any wanted posters they might have would look more like my son (if I had one, a possibility, for all I know) than me.

It was early afternoon and the town, while not quite going the whole hog and taking a siesta as they'd all be doing just fifty miles to the west, was certainly quiet. I pushed open the door and went into a dark, cool room where the blinds were drawn and a fan was softly stirring the air. There was a glass-fronted gun rack against one wall and a big corkboard covered with wanted posters and other official-looking documents, some of them yellowed by time. The room was dominated by a large desk. The top of the desk was covered with papers, quietly rustling in the draft set up by the fan.

Some of the paper wasn't moving — the sheets anchored to the desk by the biggest pair of boots I had ever seen.

I coughed and the owner of the boots, whose head was considerably more than six feet away from them, stirred. He was sitting in a chair tilted back against the wall and his hat was down over his eyes.

'Sheriff Clayhorn?'

'Yup.' The chair came forward and hit the floor with a bump that made the boards shake and rattled the guns in their case.

'My name's Dick Kelly, sheriff.' I took off my hat and approached the desk, taking out my doctored driver's licence. 'I'm working with the movie people and...'

I stopped talking as he stood up, yawned and stretched. The process took a while because he was close to seven feet tall and that's a lot of body to straighten the kinks out of. When he was fully extended, his fists almost reached the ceiling and if he'd taken a little jump there would have been no problem for him to punch a hole in it because he was big all over — those fists were the size of headlights. Somehow, the words had dried up in my throat at the sight of him — you don't chatter on when you catch your first look at the Grand Canyon.

'You were sayin'...'

'Yes, I'm...ah, with the *Giant* people and...' I couldn't help using the word although as soon as I spoke I had a sense that the joke must have already worn thin. He sat down and I could see that the chair had been specially reinforced to hold his weight. It creaked, nonetheless.

'Ok,' the sheriff said. 'So y'all an actor? So what can I do for you?'

I explained why I was there. It sounded pretty lame, a small thing to be putting to a man his size but he frowned and seemed to take it seriously. He told me to sit down, unfolded a blade on a large jack knife and began cleaning his fingernails. There was a lot of grime and he let it fall neatly into a waste paper basket.

'I saw those letters myself,' he said. 'Turned 'em over to the FBI.'

I had to prevent myself from reacting. The last thing I needed was to be brought into association with Hoover's boys. He finished with his nails and rummaged in a drawer, coming up with a block of printed forms. He spun my driver's licence around and began to write.

'FBI said it could be a concern of theirs on account of the mail being used. That's violation of federal statutes. On the other hand, they're busy and this is just a shit-kickin' li'l ol' Texas town and who cares what happens to a bunch of Hollywood faggots anyway? You get my meaning?'

I nodded. Right then, anyone critical of the FBI was ok by me.

'But here in Marfa,' Clayhorn went on, 'we take it a mite more seriously than that. This movie's gonna bring a pile of money into town now and for some time to come. We don't want anything happening to spoil this fortunate circumstance, so I'm pleased to issue you with a pistol licence, Mr Kelly. You look like a man can handle himself. Been in the service?'

'Yes, sheriff. Canadian army.'

A slip — that dismal period of my life would be on file, but Sheriff Clayhorn just clicked his tongue approvingly and went on writing. I was glad of the willing cooperation, but a bit worried about the credence being given to the death threats. I was happy enough to pack a gun and stand around looking alert, but I didn't actually want to get between James Dean and flying bullets. Clayhorn pushed my licence and the gun permit across the desk.

'Couple good gunsmiths in town. You might try Charlie Earp on Main Street. Pick yourself up a good .45 there for a reasonable price. Tell Charlie I sent you. He's got a range out back you can try the weapon at.'

'Has anyone else applied for a permit? I mean, from the movie company?'

'Yup. There's a guy looking after Miz Taylor and Mr Hudson himself has a gun. He's a nice fellow that Rock Hudson. Not used to meetin' up with a man a sight bigger'n him but he took it well. Hang on, I'll get you the name of the other guy. Don't want you two taking pot shots at each other in the dark. Here it is — Pedro Cortez — you two better get acquainted.'

I'd known a Pedro Cortez back when I fought in a mercenary army in Mexico, made my first try at Hollywood and ended up scooting to Canada chased by the IWW and some rum-runners,[35] but it's a common name. Clayhorn stuck his hand out and we shook — that is to say, he shook my hand, I could hardly have got a grip on three fingers. I was still worried.

'Could I see the letters?'

He rummaged in a drawer in the desk. 'Like I say, I sent 'em to Washington. They kept the originals but they sent me back these photocopies. You know how they do that, make photocopies?'

'No,' I said. He opened an envelope and took out three stiff sheets with blackened edges. The copies were a bit smudged and hard to read. Typewritten, the originals must have been done on a machine with an old ribbon. The messages were much the same — stop filming and get out of Marfa or you'll be sorry. *Giant* is an insult to Mexican-Americans that will not be tolerated. Carry on with this obscenity and more people than Luz Benedict and Angel Obregon will die. They were unsigned and addressed to Stevens, Edna Ferber and the scriptwriter, Fred Guiol. All that told me was the writer possibly knew how things worked in the movie business.

'Have there been any incidents? Any trouble?'

'Not a thing. Only problem I've had is with your man Mr Dean.'

'How's that?'

'He was caught driving that red convertible a tad fast over on Coltrane Road. Might possibly have had a drop to drink. My guy let him off with a caution, wanting to be cooperative like I say. Be a good idea if someone'd do his driving for him. Like you, maybe.'

I couldn't see Jimmy going for that idea. 'I'll put it to him. Ah, sheriff, have you got any...suspects?'

He laughed, making a rich sound with a fair amount of bourbon and prairie dust in it. 'Hell, no. We got a lot of people around here can write. Between you and me, I don't believe this is a colour thing.'

'No?'

'No. I'd be more worried about blackmail or kidnapping. Border's only an hour away.'

CHAPTER SEVENTEEN

I moved into the Marfa house with Dean, Hudson and Wills, occupying a small, draughty room at the back. As I expected, I spent the next few days being bored and nights getting drunk. I made two tries at ringing Louise and was told both times by members of the Sherman House staff that she was out of town. That was worrying, but fixed as I was I couldn't press for more details and it didn't seem safe to leave my number in case the FBI was hanging about. I tried to call Bobby Silk but he was in New York fixing up a deal. The world was rolling on without me.

I saw very little of Hudson and Wills who had other places of entertainment or were so tired they slept a lot. One of my jobs was shaking off the bobby-soxers. The location of the house wasn't exactly a secret, but a number of things conspired to make my task easier than you might think. In the first place, the girls were more interested in Rock Hudson than James Dean who was, at that time, just barely a star. Hudson, as I say, was something of a gadfly, and the fans quickly learned that staking out the house or following any of the known cars was no sure way to catch a glimpse of him. Also, this was 1955, and the girls interested in James Dean tended to be young and still under the control of their parents, which might make Marfa sound like Mars, but that's the way things were back then.

Dean wasn't fucking anybody — not Liz, not Carroll Baker, not Rock. By day, he was working, practising roping tricks, taking still photographs around the sets by virtue of a special arrangement he had with Stevens and the studio and scribbling in his journal. By night, he was studying how to upstage the other actors, drinking wine, smoking a little marijuana and playing the bongo drums. The Smith & Wesson .38 Combat Masterpiece I'd bought from Charlie Earp had not once cleared its chamois holster.

I hadn't seen Liz Taylor since her appearance in what everyone was now calling 'the pissing scene'. She'd been out of town for a few days, having treatment for a back complaint at a hospital in San Antonio. When I got up on the fourth morning there was a big white Plymouth parked outside the house. A shirtless Mexican in jeans and bare feet was washing the car. I walked across the street and was surprised to hear that he was whistling something classical. I can't tell Beethoven from Brahms, but he was whistling sweetly and the melody was complicated and interesting. It was almost a shocking sound to hear in Marfa — so far on the radio I'd only heard Lawrence Welk, gospel singing and some dreadful noise from a young man in Lubbock a couple of hundred miles to the north. In Texas, that made him a local.[36]

Although he was whistling and making a noise with the water and wash cloth he heard me coming, whipped around and had a pistol pointed at my chest before I'd crossed the road.

'Hey, hey, amigo,' I said. 'Take it easy. I'm on the team.'

He examined me closely before slipping the gun back into the waistband of his pants. He kept on looking at me and I kept looking at him. He was tallish for a Mexican, very lean and fit-looking and not young. There was grey in his dark hair and his face was seamed and experienced.

Recognition dawned for both of us simultaneously.

'Pedro!'

'Dick!'

It may seem remarkable, but we recognised each other after thirty years. I suppose that's a tribute to the fact that neither of us had gained much weight, both had kept our hair and teeth, and time had treated us kindly, at least in outward appearances. Of course for my part, it helped that Sheriff Clayhorn had mentioned the name Pedro Cortez and it had lodged in my head somewhere; but quite how Pedro knew me through the mists of time and the grey beard I didn't find out until we'd shaken hands, slapped backs and reminded each other of how we'd escaped from Mexico, led the good life briefly in Hollywood and split up with the law breathing down our necks in Canada.[37]

'I'd have known you anywhere, Dick,' Pedro said, 'from the look in your eyes when I pulled out the gun.'

I lit a cigarette, feigning nonchalance and remembering what a wisearse Pedro — ex-school-teacher, unwilling but adept soldier, intellectual and man-of-action — could be. I said, 'How's that?' and pulled out my gun, pointing it at the grey, grizzled hair on his chest.

He grinned. 'You were always ready to bluff or run. Now you're ready to shoot. I under-estimated you.'

I put the gun away. 'You did. How come you're washing someone else's car?'

That's the way it had always been with us — banter with more than a little bite.

'How do you know it's not my car, *Senor Dick?*'

'Elizabeth Taylor's house. I've been told one Pedro Cortez is her bodyguard and I find a greaser in jeans and bare feet slopping the soapy rag about. What else am I to think?'

Pedro laughed. 'You're right. I'm Elizabeth Taylor's bodyguard and I'm washing her car. Now what is Richard Browning doing here? Coming out of Rock Hudson and James Dean's house at eight o'clock in the morning? Don't tell me you've turned fag, Dick?'

That was Pedro — very sharp and always ready to catch you on the hop. I'd forgotten that I'd never won a verbal battle with him, ever, and here he was again, with only a few words exchanged and he had me on the defensive.

'Er, the name's not Browning, Pedro. It's Kelly. Dick Kelly, and I'm bodyguarding James Dean.'

Pedro began washing the car again, moving the cloth rhythmically across the duco and humming to himself. I knew what that meant — he was thinking, and Pedro's thinking had only one end in view — to put Pedro Cortez in the driver's seat. I was beginning to wish I hadn't crossed the road. On the other hand, his quick draw had been very impressive and if these aggrieved Mexican-Americans were going to be gunning for our stars and meal-tickets I definitely wanted Pedro on my side.

'So you're not the Richard Browning of Sherman Oaks? Not the guy who helped some gangster escape from the FBI a while back? Not the guy with the cute Aussie wife with the mean forehand and a way with horses?'

There was no point in fencing with Pedro. Thirty years hadn't blunted or changed him — he had all the moves.

'No,' I said, 'not him. And I suppose you're not the guy I dropped off just this side of the Canadian border with only a Thompson machine gun for luggage?'

Pedro laughed. 'That's a long time ago, Dick. I don't really remember. It doesn't sound like me. Weighing it all up, I'd say the man who can still use his own name, even when he takes a dumb-ass job like bodyguarding, is ahead. What d'you think?'

'You've missed some dust on that fender.'

He laughed. 'Same old Dick. Well, we'll have to get together for a few tequilas some time when we're not minding our clients' expensive asses. How much is Dean paying you?'

The subject hadn't come up and I was beginning to wonder myself. Free bed and board was all very well, but I was starting to dip into my capital for the luxuries and I didn't know where any more money was coming from.

'Enough,' I said.

'Means not enough. Me, I'm getting three hundred a week. Not great, but makes me probably the best-paid Mexican around here. And the work certainly isn't hard, is it?'

My mind was working fast now. I'd put myself in Pedro's hands well and truly. If he wanted to look on the ball and make a reputation for himself, all he had to do was lift a phone and call the FBI. But I had a strong sense that he wasn't interested in doing that. In fact, now that he'd won the sparring match he was looking a little uneasy as he splashed, soaped and wiped. I wondered why.

I probed. 'You a US citizen these days, Pedro?'

'Sure thing. For twenty years. You?'

I nodded. 'That LA thing. There's nothing to it. My wife's got a lawyer sorting it out. I'm just kind of lying low for a while till it blows over. You live down here now?'

He shook his head.

'Where?'

'Here and there.'

A woman appeared on the porch at the front of the house and beckoned. Pedro had his head down polishing chrome and didn't notice.

'You're wanted.' I said.

He looked up, saw the woman and swore in Spanish. 'Look, Dick,' he said quickly. 'I got to finish up here and drive her ladyship. I'll see you later. We should talk.'

I agreed and walked back to my base, wondering why I was so sure Pedro wouldn't sell me out. We'd never exactly been friends and from one point of view — possibly his — I hadn't treated him well back in the old days. He had no cause to love me. There could only be one reason — he was up to something and making trouble for me would only make more trouble for him. Intriguing, and something to think about while I hung around watching Jimmy steal scenes and worried about what Louise was doing and what lay ahead of me once shooting this big piece of soap opera was finished.

James Dean was nervous. Anyone who'd read the book or the script knew that the scene where Jett Rink strikes oil was potentially the most impactful moment in the whole show. No one knew it better than Dean and, as we got ready to drive out to the spot where they'd set up the oil rig, he amazed me by tossing over the keys to his car.

'You drive, Dick.'

I caught the keys, just. 'What's the matter? I thought you hated to have anyone drive you.'

'I do, but this is different. Just do it, ok?'

I'd learned that the only way to handle him was not to knuckle under. I jiggled the keys. 'Not sure I'm being paid for driving. In fact, I'm not sure I'm being paid at all. What exactly is the deal there? Should I go ask Stevens about it?'

He looked sheepish. 'No, don't do that. I'm paying you myself. Two fifty a week. Ok?'

'Let's go.'

Who knows why he wanted it that way. Perhaps he couldn't swing it with Stevens for his bodyguard to go on the payroll; maybe he didn't want anyone to *know* he had a bodyguard. With James Dean, it was hard to keep your footing. I made myself one pledge on that drive — not to be around him when he eventually became the biggest star in the Hollywood sky which everyone said he would be. It was LA to a palm tree that he'd be insufferable.

The set-up for the scene was simple enough. The oil rig was erected on a bare patch of boggy land that Jett Rink had called Little Reata to get right up the nose of Bick Benedict, who was pro-cattle and anti-oil. Bick's sister, Luz, had left the land to Jett as some kind of compensation for the shitty way the Benedicts had always treated him. The notion was that Jett had spent what little money he had on drilling for oil and had come up dry a number of times. Out of cash, this was his last throw of the dice. Pure Hollywood.

A barrel of fake oil, stuff that would wash off easier than the real thing, was buried underground. It was under pressure and a valve would be opened at the right minute to send the gusher skywards. The timing had to be right. I've heard that James Dean only appears on screen in *Giant* for about twenty minutes[38], but he certainly made the most of them. One thing was obvious even from watching the shoots for a few days at a distance the way I did. Dean was the only really convincing character in the cast. This was partly because his role had some meat in it, but it was more than that. I've thought about it and my conclusion is this — Jett Rink was supposed to be a workman, someone who'd done things with his hands all his life. Dean made you believe that. The others were just actors. Rock Hudson looked as much like a cattle baron as Mickey Rooney. Come to think of it, Rooney would have played it better.

Dean sat in the convertible with his hat tilted forward mumbling to himself. When we reached the place Dean jumped out and began walking around, smoking, kicking up dust and staring into the sky. George Stevens was forced to walk with him, puffing on his pipe, gesticulating, trying to get a line through to genius. I did the obligatory look around to see if there was any politically-motivated crazy in sight although how you could tell with all the technicians, labourers and hangers-on milling about I didn't know. There was a lot of equipment to check, safety devices to test and routines to run through. Eventually Dean stood stock still, had a last drag on his cigarette and a swallow of water, took off his hat, threw it down on his chair and marched towards the rig.

Out of all the thousands of movie scenes I've witnessed being played and shot I think it's the one that sticks clearest in my mind. All the mechanics worked smoothly and Dean played it perfectly — not much movement, no over-statement, just pure physical presence and emotional power. He *was* Jett Rink, he *had* struck oil and he *was* going to have more money than Jordan Benedict had ever dreamed of. There was silence on the set when Stevens said 'Cut.' Dean was standing there, covered in black goo. He hadn't finished by a long chalk — he had to make his crazy, halfdrunk, lurching run to the oil-blackened truck and drive off as if he was running the truck straight to hell, but everyone broke into loud clapping and I admit that I joined in, clapping as loudly as anyone.

Dean lifted his head and grinned. 'Anyone got a cigarette?' he mumbled.

There are no words required when you do something extraordinary — shoot a par round of golf, play an unblemished set of tennis, score a possible on the rifle range — you just have to sit there and feel good, possibly wishing the feeling would last and last. That's what James Dean did in the car after the day's work. He didn't talk, he didn't even smoke. He just sat and thought his thoughts. I didn't interrupt him — he'd earned the right to his time with himself.

The day was still hot, although driving the convertible with the top down was breezy. Dean had got cleaned up and was wearing fresh clothes, the first I'd seen him in since getting to Marfa. After a while he started to hum to himself and I judged he'd done enough meditating on his own greatness.

'Want to drive?' I said.

'No, what I really want to do is fuck.'

'Must be plenty of candidates.'

'Yeah, I guess so.'

He lit a cigarette and went quiet. Maybe I was going to have a busy night for a change. We turned into our street and I parked the very dusty red convertible. Hudson and Wills had drivers who picked them up and dropped them off, but the house looked closed up and empty. We got out of the car and walked towards the porch. I had my foot on the step when I heard the first shot. It was almost forty years since I'd done the training but it stays with you — I threw myself to the ground, dragging Dean with me, as two more whistled above our heads and thudded into the timber porch rail.

CHAPTER EIGHTEEN

You won't read of this incident in any of the numerous biographies of James Dean because we didn't mention it to anyone then, and this is the first time I've spoken about it since. Dean went along with that when I pointed out a few things to him. First off, I hustled him into the house. He was scared, trembling a little but he handled himself pretty well. I didn't hear any cars starting up or driving off, so there was a chance the gunman was still around. We lay low in the house for a while. The street was quiet at that time of day and I suppose the shots could have been taken for backfires. The reports weren't loud which was an interesting fact in itself. In any case, no one came to investigate.

After a decent interval, I unshipped the .38 and slipped out onto the porch, feeling fairly safe. A few cars had driven by and no shooter in his right mind would stick around that long. Anyway, who'd want to shoot the bodyguard? As I've indicated, my military experience has been much more extensive than I've ever welcomed. I was an infantryman and sniper in France in 1918, a platoon leader in a Mexican mercenary army after that and in the Canadian army tank corps. I also survived some pretty dangerous semi-military exercises in the Queensland jungle in 1944.[39] The upshot of all this is that something about those shots rang bells with me. They were fired with a military precision.

No one took a pot shot at me on the porch, so I holstered the .38 and took a look at the upright where the bullets had struck. It was a solid piece of timber about eight inches square and the marksman had achieved a good, tight pattern — three shots, all lodged within an inch or two of each other, spreading over no more than twenty-five square inches. I went down the steps and retraced the walk Dean and I had made. At the time when the shots were fired, I would have had my foot on the first of three steps that led to the porch. That meant the bullets missed my head by about ten inches. Since James Dean was a good six inches shorter than yours truly and a few feet behind me at that moment, he had as much chance of being struck by those bullets as Paul Robeson had of hitting a high C.

Dean came out onto the porch with a lit reefer in one hand and a bottle of beer in the other. I called him down to where I was and explained things to him slowly and clearly. It was obvious that his intention was to blot himself out for a time, but at that moment he could *comprende* pretty well.

'Some kinda stunt?' he said.

'What it looks like.'

'Why the fuck?'

'I'm not a detective, just a bodyguard.'

He took a suck on the bottle and offered me the cigarette. I refused. 'You did pretty good, Dick. You moved fast. You know, I've heard about things like this — actors setting up death threats. Maybe this was all a studio stunt, what d'you think?'

'I don't know. I saw the letters, but I guess anyone could have written them. You, even.'

He giggled. Yes, sir, I reckon I could have. But I didn't. I hate all that crap. You saw what I can do out at the oil rig today. I don't need stunts and stuff like that. I'm the best goddamn actor who ever...' He stopped and looked again at the bullet marks. 'You figure someone in the studio could do this — for the publicity?'

I shrugged. 'It's possible.'

'By Christ, if I could find out who it was I'd have them by the nuts. I could threaten to expose them unless they re-wrote my contract.'

I was thinking fast. I had my suspicions about who the marksman could be and, if I was right, I could see my bodyguarding job evaporating. But Dean was holding out the prospect of an extension.

'I could look into it,' I said. 'I used to hold a PI licence. It's a while back but I guess I still remember the moves.'

Dean reached up and thumped me on the shoulder. 'Why don't you do that, Dick? I'd sure be grateful. Meantime, we'd better keep this our secret, huh? Tell you what though, I'm going to get me some pictures of these fucking bullet holes.'

He put the beer down on the porch rail and rushed inside and returned with one of his cameras. He fiddled with lenses and a light meter and took a series of photographs of the porch post. It sounds ridiculous and it was, but he was very earnest about it and I guess he got some great shots. He was as happy as a kid as he went back inside, trailing marijuana smoke and humming to himself.

I drank the beer and waited until he was gone before taking out a clasp knife and digging into the wood for the bullets. They were flattened and bent out of shape by the impact although they hadn't penetrated very far. I don't know a lot about ammunition, but I could tell that it was cheap, low calibre stuff, suitable for jack rabbits, not the sort of thing you'd use for a serious assassination.

Dean settled down with his pot, beer and his journal, no doubt writing an account of how brilliant he'd been on the set that day. I said I'd be back with hamburgers and fries at six o'clock and he gave me a happy, halfstoned wave. I crossed the road and went down the driveway to the back of the house Elizabeth Taylor was occupying. It was locked up tight but your average suburban house is no fortress to a man with a good clasp knife. I slipped the catch on the back door and was inside within seconds. A quick scout around revealed that three people were in residence, Liz, her maid and her bodyguard.

Pedro's room was at the back, close to the kitchen and the garage. The door was locked but the key was on the lintel — too easy. It took me about three minutes to find a battered hockshop portable Remington typewriter with a faded ribbon and a box of Lone Star .22 long rifle ammunition with five rounds missing. I kept an ear cocked for sounds outside and did a thorough search of Pedro's possessions. He had a presentable suitcase and some good clothes and shoes that showed signs of careful maintenance but a lot of wear and cleaning. A collection of business cards in various names, two driver's licences with chequebooks to match and a batch of faded newspaper clippings showed pretty clearly what Pedro's life had been since we'd parted up on the Canadian border all those years ago — in the words of the song, he'd grifted from Maine to Albuquerque.[40]

It made me sad to look at it and partly the pity was for myself. My own life hadn't been so very different until recently. I was filled with a fierce desire to get out of Texas, to return to Louise and our thriving business in Hollywood, to put down solid roots while there was still time. I heard a car door slam and hurried through the house to look out a front window. The Plymouth had pulled up and Elizabeth Taylor was approaching the house along with her maid and a couple of people I vaguely recognised — a continuity girl and a props man. Pedro eased the car up towards the garage. I scooted back to his room, replaced the key and closed the door behind me.

I was sitting on his bed with the .38 in my hand when he entered the room carrying a rifle in one hand and a bottle in the other.

'Put the rifle on the floor, *amigo*,' I said. 'What's in the bottle?'

He propped the rifle against the wall, moving very slowly, keeping his hands in plain view. As he'd said, Pedro knew how nervous I get around firearms.

'It's brandy, Dick.'

I reached out and took the bottle. 'Good idea. Why don't you go into the kitchen and get some mixers? Then we can have a little quiet *conversacion*.'

Pedro told me all about his life in America. He'd got citizenship by marrying a woman fifteen years older than himself and then got the surprise of his life when she ran off with a younger man. He could still laugh about it. After that it had been mainly card- playing and scams and cons and stings of one kind or another until he enlisted in the marines. He served in the Pacific with some distinction but then found peacetime life hard to adjust to. He'd done some time inside for fraud and false pretences, running an illegal gaming house and living on immoral earnings.

'If I was becoming a pimp I figured I might as well go back to Hollywood,' he said. 'If I'd known you were around and in such a good way of business I'd have looked you up, Dick. Asked you for a job maybe.'

'Doing what? We only teach honest things —like tennis and golf and riding...'

Our eyes drifted to the rifle leaning against the wall.

'And shooting. I was always a great shot, Dick. Better than you and you weren't bad.'

'I remember. That's one of the reasons I came over here. You got a nice tight pattern. Which brings us to the here and now.'

Pedro told me that he'd tried to get acting work with no luck. He landed a job as a security man with Warners and had wangled a place on the location crew.

'At a lousy thirty-five bucks a week plus allowances,' he said. 'I sized up the situation and figured out a way to get a little more.'

'You sure did. What were you going to do next? Put a tarantula in Liz's bed?'

He laughed. 'Who knows? This could be a sweet deal for us, Dick?'

But I already had my own sweet deal worked out, sweet enough anyway. 'Definitely not, Pedro and you're going to stop as of now or I blow the whistle on you. Don't be greedy. Be like me. We can both play bodyguard until this thing is over.'

He took a big swig of brandy. His eyes glittered. He was well on the way to being drunk and I could see wheels turning in his brain. I've seen the type often — they become addicted to scheming, manoeuvring the suckers.

'Sure,' he said. 'I'll get some more ice.'

While he was gone I fed a sheet of paper into the typewriter and tapped out the alphabet and the quick brown fox with two fingers. I took the sheet and put it on the bed beside me. Then I put the rifle on top of it and lit a cigarette. When Pedro got back with a bowl of ice I was tossing the flattened slugs in my hand. He stared. 'What the hell are you doing?'

'Insurance,' I said. 'Just in case you think it might be a good idea to put me in to the Feds. Lotta evidence here, and Jimmy Dean's got a peachy set of photos of the porch post. Threatening letters, shooting with intent, serious charges. D'we understand each other?'

He sat down and built two more big drinks. Like me, Pedro was one of those men who didn't look his age, but every now and then that mask of youthfulness can slip. His slipped now.

I raised my drink. 'Cheer up,' I said. 'Maybe I can find you a job at Sherman House. We're thinking of teaching card tricks.'

CHAPTER NINETEEN

THINGS became rather quiet around Marfa after that, at least as far as I was concerned. The filming seemed to be going well, despite lots of confrontations between James Dean and George Stevens and the development of a very healthy mutual dislike between Dean and Hudson. With my help, Jimmy managed a few startling practical jokes, like the time we parked the red convertible in the middle of a herd of cows not long before the cameras were due to roll. Irritating but harmless stuff that Dean had no trouble getting away with. The oil rig scene had convinced everybody that he was the goods and, although that may have been a trifle uncomfortable for Hudson and Taylor, it was reassuring to Stevens and others who'd sunk their money in the picture. The atmosphere on the set became more relaxed and evening and weekend parties became common.

Of course Pedro and I didn't let on about the evaporation of the death threats. We kept right on bodyguarding but I was certainly putting less and less time and attention into it although I tried to make it look good. I even reported on my activities to Sheriff Clayhorn once in a while just to show I was keeping the faith. Pedro was keen to stage another stunt to keep the ball rolling but I vetoed that. Dean was getting more and more into his character, wandering around in his dirty clothes, playing with a lariat and mumbling to himself. He seemed to have forgotten his plan of getting the moral drop on the studio, but just as if the plan was still active, he only had to be asked two or three times before he'd quite cheerfully write out my pay cheque.

Eventually I got through to Louise who told me she'd gone to San Francisco to hire a lawyer.

'Why go to 'Frisco?' I complained. 'LA's crawling with lawyers.'

'That's the trouble. Bobby says they can't be trusted and that it's better for a lawyer from the state capital to deal with the FBI.'

Bobby Silk was always full of shit — he was so devious he looked clever much of the time but I'd known him to be just plain dumb. The capital of California is Sacramento, not San Francisco. Louise couldn't be expected to know that but Bobby could, or could he? At once I suspected that Bobby had set Louise up with a lawyer he could handle and for his own reasons.

'So who did you get and what does he charge?'

'His name's Frank Brennan and I don't know what he charges. He hasn't billed me yet, but he seems to know a lot about the government and all that.'

Brennan? It didn't ring a bell. Bobby Silk was one of the most anti-semitic people I'd ever met and it would be just like him to hire an Irish lawyer... I realised that was crazy thinking and I was full of frustration at being unable to do anything from where I was.

'Give me his number, Louise. I'll call him.'

'Is that safe? I mean, you're still a fugitive. I wish I knew where you were Dick.'

Right then, I was sitting in a comfortable suburban living room with a bottle of Coors beer in my hand, ready to watch the television news. I felt as safe as Ike in the White House. Louise gave me the number and I wrote it down, planning to put this Brennan through the ringer a little, see if he knew the FBI from the DMV.[41] I told Louise that I was fine and that it would all be sorted out soon. She said she missed me and I said the same. We both meant it. I had a vision of her strong, athletic legs stepping out of her stockings and of the way she moved towards me, unfastening her bra and teasing her nipples... If I watched the news I don't remember what it was about — probably the same old stuff about victory being just around the corner in Korea and what devils those Soviets were.

I phoned Brennan two days later when the visions started to become more frequent and to get too much for me. I was a little drunk at the time of the call. I suppose I expected a brogue and blarney but he spoke in a clipped, educated Eastern accent.

'Mr Browning? I'm very glad to hear from you. It helps to make personal contact. I expect you'd like a report on how your case is progressing?'

'Not really,' I said, 'I'd just like to know how things stand now. What've the Feds got on me? How serious are they? And how do I get out of it?'

'You're very direct but I can see your point. As of now, there are no formal charges against you, but I've been given to understand that the offences you *could* face are serious.'

'Like?'

'Harbouring a fugitive, obstructing officers in the execution of their duties, assisting a fugitive to escape lawful custody ...'

'They all sound a bit Mickey Mouse to me.'

'And various offences under the Immigration Act.'

Those'd be the ones with the teeth — they could do almost anything to you under the Immigration Act, including lock you up or deport you. Especially someone like me who'd had a dubious immigration status for years before acquiring citizenship. Brennan could tell he had my attention.

'They want to deal, Mr Browning.'

'About what?'

'I don't know, but my impression is that if they can get certain assurances from you, your position will be more favourable.'

Lawyer talk. What the hell did it mean? I tried to think my way through it but I was in a nasty spot. If I told Brennan about the mob money behind Sherman House and how it had given them the leverage to put the screws on me, where would that leave me and Louise with the hoods, even if we could square things with the FBI? On the other hand, the Feds were the present and immediate problem. The trick would be to play one threat off against the other and squeak out somehow in one piece. I wasn't sure that I was up to it. It was a lawyerly kind of job, but could I trust Brennan? Who could I find to check on him? Could I trust anyone to run the check? I was getting confused. Brennan's voice was calm and re-assuring.

'It's a complicated matter and a challenging one for me. I understand that you're a valued client of Mr Silkstein and I assure you I'm doing all I can to achieve a satisfactory outcome. It would be helpful if we could meet, Mr Browning.'

That remark about Bobby should have alerted me, but I was on my own in Texas, randy and missing my wife and seduced by that firm, professional Morocco-bound voice.

'I'm in Texas,' I said.

'A big state. The biggest, I fancy. Where in Texas, exactly?'

As I say, I was drunk and lonely when I started the conversation and a little more drunk by this point. 'Town called Marfa. Don't ask what it's near, 'cos it ain't near nothin', as they'd probably say down here.'

'I'm sure I can find it on the map. I'll be down there as soon as I can manage. Three days at the most. Your wife is very concerned, are you all right for funds?'

Another warning I didn't heed. A lawyer offering money is like a politician offering truth. I was in a mood to be comforted and didn't read the signs. 'I'm OK. You really think this thing can be fixed up?'

'I'm sure of it. Stay put, Mr Browning. I'll see you soon.'

The phone went dead and before I could ponder on what had transpired, Jimmy Dean came bounding into the room. 'Hey, Dick, we're going downtown for ribs — Dennis and me and some of the boys. Come along.'

'You kids don't want an old feller like me.'

'The hell we don't. The chicks in this town are starting to drive us nuts. We need some mature protection. C'mon, Dick. You're too tanked to drive, I can see that. But you're on duty.'

James Dean, you have to remember was only twenty-five and Dennis Hopper was even younger. Neither had done military service or had the sorts of experience that bring maturity — in many ways they acted younger than their years. So it wasn't unusual for them to spend a night in the town, eating hamburgers or spare ribs, drinking spiked coca-cola, and flirting with the female Marfans like a couple of teenagers. I found it all very boring, especially when they played jungle music on the jukebox at top volume. My job was to keep some of the young men of the town, who got jealous at the attention their girlfriends paid the movie stars, from becoming violent. It wasn't too hard. I look a lot more fierce than I am and a few casual displays of the .38 helped.

I sobered up as the young people got drunk and I managed to whittle the party down to three girls in the end. Hopper took two of them back to his hotel, which left me, Jimmy and a junior college sophomore home on her vacation. Her name was Sara-May Tardbetter and she was staying at her aunt's farmhouse a few miles out of town. Nothing would do but Jimmy would escort her home, but Jimmy was too drunk to drive. I steered the convertible along a series of dusty back roads until we finally reached a pocket handkerchief farm in the middle of nowhere.

'Reminds me of home,' Jimmy said. 'How about we set on the porch a spell?'

They sat on the porch and I sat in the car, smoking and wondering when I'd next hear from lawyer Brennan. They sat a long time and Jimmy was almost sober himself by the time he climbed into the passenger's seat.

'Nice girl,' he said.

'Maybe you should marry her.'

He laughed so hard he was sick all down the side of the car.

Saturday night was spent in pretty much the same way except that I heard doors opening and closing out at the Tardbetter farm and I gathered that Jimmy and Sara-May hadn't spent all their time on the porch. Dean was more sober this time and he took over the wheel for the drive back to Marfa.

'What's she studying at college?' I asked.

He giggled. 'What all boneheads study, what I studied 'fore I switched to drama — physical fucking education.'

I gathered from his tone that we wouldn't be seeing a lot more of Sara-May.

Sunday morning at the Dean-Hudson-Wills-Kelly place was spent recovering from hangovers and waiting until it was time for a beer or two with lunch.

In the afternoon Jimmy got a phone call from Stevens calling him to an urgent meeting at the hotel the director was staying at in town. I was getting tired of my mock bodyguarding role by this time and I made an excuse not to go. Hanging around film sets, though boring enough, does have its compensations in the way of attractive women to look at. Hotel hallways are another thing altogether. Hudson was going to the meeting and he had some muscleman in tow so Jimmy went with them.

Pedro was washing that Plymouth again and not looking happy about it. I sauntered over to share a beer with him and kill some time. He pressed me for some details on how I planned to get back to respectability in Hollywood and I wasn't able to provide any. He glanced across at Dean's car.

'You could spend a little time on that car. It looks like it's been used to round up hogs on a dirt farm.'

'That's the way he likes it. Fits his image.'

Pedro nodded. 'He sure is scruffy. You reckon he's going to stay like that?'

'I doubt it. The script calls for him to become a tycoon in tails later on. I reckon you won't see him out of a tuxedo for a while.'

Pedro shook his head. 'Actors.'

I examined myself in one of the Plymouth's side mirrors. I fancied there was more grey than before in my hair and beard and, even though I'd been wearing a hat, the Texas sun had given me a weatherbeaten look. I doubted that Louise would recognise me — a worrying thought. I went back to the house, had another beer and tried to catch up on some of the sleep I'd been losing. My mind was burdened and it took me a long time to get to sleep. When I finally did I must have gone deep and long because it was dark outside when I woke up. That didn't worry me, what worried me was the feel of the business end of a pistol poking into my earhole and the smell of sweat, tobacco and whisky.

A man was sitting on my bed holding a long-barrelled Colt .45 on me. In the gloom I could scarcely see him and from his stink I didn't want to.

'Where's Dean at?' he said in a harsh, whining Texas accent. 'I'm planning to kill him and I don't mind including you.'

CHAPTER TWENTY

'HE's not here,' I stammered.

'I know he ain't here. I done looked through the house real thorough. I looked in that room of his and seen all that devil-worship stuff he's got in there.'

'What?'

'Them drums and them books and records.'

I knew that Jimmy had some books about the occult, harmless mindless stuff about tarot cards and such. 'Jesus,' I said, 'that's not...'

The Colt bit deep into my ear. 'You're the same stamp. You just used the Lord's name in vain. That buys you a bullet.'

I could feel the warmth of the blood as it welled in my ear and dripped down the side of my face. 'Wait, wait. I don't understand this. Who are you?'

'I'm a God-fearing Texan been watching your Mister Dean these past few weeks. Been watching him real close. You know one thing I've noticed?'

He was clearly mad, partly drunk and, from the sound of his voice, quite old. If I could just get myself into a position that would give me some leverage I thought I might have a chance at him. But I was well and truly pinned down and the only thing to do was play along. People don't shoot you while in the middle of talking to you. Not usually.

'No,' I said, wriggling a bit, trying to get an arm free of the sheet. I was acutely conscious that I was naked and that my own pistol was a long way off. 'What have you noticed?'

'Lie still. He don't never go to church.'

I almost blasphemed again and might have lost my life there and then if I had. I managed to bite the expression back.

'He goes when he's at home in Los Angeles,' I said. 'It's just that down here...'

'What kinda church does he go to?'

He had me there. Naming the wrong one was likely to be a very bad move. Marfa was full of churches, different varieties of Baptist and Methodist and lots of others I'd never heard of. My chances of coming out with the right brand were nil.

'I don't know. I think he goes to a lot of churches. He's still searching...'

'Don't give me that. That's a lie. Lyin's a sin too — a very bad sin.'

I realised that I was in the hands of a true religious maniac, one of the most dangerous human specimens in existence, because such people hate almost everybody and feel totally justified in everything they do. This puts them in another dimension from chaps like me, who like most people and are never quite sure what's the right thing to do. Except survive. I concentrated on that thought.

'I'm sure Mr Dean would be glad to listen to what you have to say. And I'm sure you can persuade him to attend the church of your choice. What's the time? Is it too late for a service tonight?'

The gun bit me again. 'Church is in the morning. Right after sun-up.'

Probably complete with serpents and talking in tongues. 'Of course. That's a right shame. Yes, well, perhaps next Sunday...'

'Ain't goin' to be no next Sunday for that sinner. I seen the way the girls go after him. Decent, god-fearin' girls until he come along with his Devil ways. They like to worship him, and the Lord says "Thou shalt have no Gods but me." That's what the Lord says.'

Crazier and crazier and now with a note of sexual jealousy. The brew was getting more potent by the second. I was sweating and I had a bursting bladder, a bad feeling when you're gripped by fear.

'What about "vengeance is mine"? What about that, Mr...'

'Tardbetter, Duane Tardbetter. I sees you know the name.'

I couldn't help reacting. I twitched and let out a breath I must have been holding for a long time. At that point I was just about ready to give up. If he'd been watching events out at the farm he'd have gathered plenty of fuel to stoke his insane fire, and he'd be able to hold me just as guilty as James Dean. I'd always wanted to die in bed, but not like this. My eyes had adjusted to the gloom and by swivelling them I could just get a look at the Colt. It was an old-fashioned model, possibly badly maintained. I certainly couldn't smell any fresh oil on it and my senses were tuned fine for survival. Still, his hand was steady and it would have required more nerve than I possess to take a chance on a mis-fire. I forced myself to relax and tried to work my hand up under the pillow. Just maybe...but I had to keep him talking.

'What do you want me to do, Mr Tardbetter? You must want something or you would've just shot me where I lay. And how about that verse I just quoted you?'

'The Devil can quote scripture. Happens all the time in them Jew and Catholic churches and them places where the niggers jump about. What I want's simple enough — I want to put a bullet in that heathen laid his filthy hands on my kinswoman. Can you understand that?'

I was desperate and said the first thing that came into my head, probably triggered by the remark I'd made to Jimmy the night before. 'I do. But my understanding is that Mr Dean and Miss Tardbetter have an arrangement. Why, they're as good as engaged.'

It was his turn to react. He started, almost flinched and the metal was out of my ear. It was the best chance I was ever going to get. I heaved off the bed, lifting legs, body and arms in one desperate lunge. Tardbetter was a heavy man I discovered, but my strength was quadrupled by desperation. He toppled sideways to the floor. I jumped off the bed and took a quick kick at him, connecting, but only lightly with a bare foot. His grip on the pistol had slipped but he hadn't lost it altogether and I could tell I wouldn't have time for another shot. My clothes were lying over a chair near the door and the .38 in its holster was hooked over the chair underneath them. I sprang in that direction, made a grab but missed. My hand tangled in my shirt and the chair fell over.

Tardbetter fired and the bullet smashed into the wall. I yelled and ran — out into the hallway, heading for the back of the house. Two more bullets zinged by me as I made the turn, banging my knee painfully on the corner. I was in the kitchen, clawing at the back door. I remembered Pedro's rifle and ammunition. I'd left them in the garage. If only I could get there. I wrenched the door open and stumbled down the steps into the backyard as the big Colt boomed twice again and glass broke somewhere. I tripped on the bottom step, turned my ankle agonisingly, sprawled my length and scrambled along on all fours, desperately seeking some cover. Tardbetter was slow coming down the steps and I fancied I could hear his heavy breathing as I frantically tried to crawl towards the garage. A shot ploughed up grass and dirt in front of me, throwing it into my eyes and blinding me. I knew I wasn't going to make it to the rifle and it wouldn't matter if I did because I couldn't see anything. There was dirt in my mouth too, as if I was dead and buried already.

I managed to roll behind a low hedge but I knew it wasn't any use. The hedge wouldn't hide me or stop a bullet. *Why didn't somebody come to investigate the shots? Were they all in church?* Then I heard the sound of metal on metal and I knew that Tardbetter was re-loading the six-shooter. I tried to stand in order to charge him — not courage, just animal instinct to survive. My ankle gave way and I fell, whimpering with the pain and fear to the ground. This was it. I'd survived Kaiser Wilhelm II, Tojo and the Imperial Japanese Army, the FBI, irate husbands, Howard Hughes, Errol Flynn and Lucky Luciano and I was going to be killed in a Texas backyard by a religious maniac. I heard the cylinder of the Colt slam home and I closed my eyes.

The next thing I heard was the crunching sound of wood on bone and a harsh sigh like steam escaping from a boiler. Then something metallic hit the ground and exploded. I thought for an instant that I was back at the Somme, among the mines and mud and that I'd triggered an explosive that had ruled the bottom line for me. Then I heard Pedro's voice.

'It's all right, Dick. I've knocked him cold. You can come out now.'

I crawled from behind the hedge, tried to stand and fell down again.

'Are you wounded?' Pedro asked.

I blinked frantically, trying to clear the blood and grit. As if through a smokescreen, I saw him standing over Tardbetter, who was sprawled in the dirt. Pedro held a baseball bat casually in one hand, as if he'd just hit a homer. Relief flooded through me as I coughed and spat to clear my mouth.

'I'm not shot I don't think,' I croaked. 'I've buggered my ankle. I can't seem to stand up.'

'You might say thank you.'

'Thanks...' I was buck naked, embarrassed and bleeding from scratches and scrapes. I tried again to stand and fainted clean away.

CHAPTER TWENTY-ONE

I heard the police siren and saw the cops arrive and mill about just as if I was watching the action on a movie screen. I was suffering some kind of physical and mental paralysis that allowed me to observe events but not participate in them. It must have the been brought on by the shock of almost having my cheque cancelled by a raving religious lunatic with a frontier Colt. Other people arrived — neighbours, Chill Wills, a doctor. Somebody threw a blanket over me. Pedro was doing most of the talking. He accused Duane Tardbetter of being the writer of threatening letters and the man who'd taken a pot shot at James Dean. He even escorted one of the cops around the side of the house, no doubt to show him the bullets in the porch post.

I wanted to contradict all of this but I simply couldn't speak. The doctor inspected my lacerated ear and damaged ankle.

'Lost some blood,' he said. 'Not too much. Ankle's sprained most likely, not broke. He'll be OK.'

As a healer he was evidently of the leave-it-alone-and-it'll-get-better school. This is a philosophy I generally favour myself, but I like to have the option. He strapped the ankle and hurt me so much I managed to get out a couple of words.

'Anyone got a drop of whisky?'

Someone produced a flask and I took a swig which cleared my vision and fully restored my speech. I pointed to the other casualty.

'What about him?'

The doctor turned his attention to Tardbetter, who was lying peacefully on his back, snoring. The doctor lifted his eyelids and made a few other rudimentary examinations.

'Out cold. No concussion. He'll be OK.'

A great man to have around. They could have used him at the Little Big Horn. He was a great diagnostician too, almost as soon as he spoke, Tardbetter's bloodshot eyes fluttered open and the first thing he would have seen was me, taking another pull on the flask. Maybe he thought he was in hell, where the sinners all got a drink and the Christians went dry, because he began to weep.

'Where am I?' he whimpered. 'What's happenin'?'

For an answer, one of the sheriff's men leaned down and clamped a pair of handcuffs around his wrists. This was long before all that Miranda nonsense came in.[42] The deputy said, 'You're under arrest, Duane. How come you been carrying on in this here crazy fashion? You been at the moonshine agin?'

'I'm a sick man,' Tardbetter said. He looked across at me and held out his manacled hands entreatingly.

'I didn't hurt you none, did I, mister?'

'Not your fault you didn't. You were trying to shoot me.'

His eyes went narrow and cunning. 'How many shots did that greaser say I get off out front?'

I'd forgotten. 'Three or four.'

'You hear that, Billy Lee? You ever heard of Duane Tardbetter shootin' a rifle, missing a target the size of a man, firing three or four times?'

The deputy shook his head. 'Never did. That's a pure fact.'

'Right,' Tardbetter said, 'ain't possible.'

'You were drunk when you were shooting at me. Maybe you were drunk then as well.'

'Never happened.' He looked about to deny that he'd taken a drop of liquor in his life either, but I held up the flask invitingly.

'Care for a drink now?'

His hands shot out and I tossed the flask to him. I was in a ticklish spot. I was sure the studio wouldn't want Dean's romancing of Sara-May to become the talk of the town. No percentage in it, but it was hard to explain Duane Tardbetter's actions without reference to it, other than the way Pedro was going about it and that had a lot of drawbacks, including the fact that it was a pack of lies. I decided to fall back on my injuries and shocked state and await developments while Tardbetter drained the last drops of whisky.

Pedro came back with the other deputy and a third cop, a small guy with a squeaky voice, had got rid of the gawkers and was comforting a couple of upset suburbanites. Chill Wills had gone inside and the doctor went away looking for other victims to reassure. Marfa's law enforcement officers seemed to be graded according to height. The man who'd been with Pedro was taller than the one who'd stayed with Tardbetter and me and he seemed to have the authority for the moment — on that basis there was no doubt who'd have the final say.

'Guess we'd all better take a ride downtown and see what the sheriff has to say about this. Got to tell you that discharging of firearms inside city limits is a serious offence, Duane.'

'Didn't use t'be, Clyde,' Tardbetter said.

Clyde shifted his tobacco plug to the other side of his mouth. 'That's the truth. Times have sure changed. You kin ride with Billy-Lee and Mr Cortez here. I'd like to get acquainted with Mr Kelly. That's after he gets some clothes on.'

It's uncomfortable enough, riding in a police car with a splitting headache and a throbbing ankle and trying to remember what assumed name you're using, without worrying about other people's inventions. I wondered how long Pedro would stick to the story about Duane doing the letter-writing and shooting. The shooting he might have been up to, but somehow I doubted that he could use a typewriter with the same facility. I also wondered if Pedro had got rid of the machine and just how far I ought to back him up — another way of saying when I should leave him high and dry. Always remembering that he knew who I was and why I was hiding behind cows and horses in this god-forsaken part of the world.

My ankle had swollen up too far for me to pull on my pants, so I was wearing a shirt, boxer shorts and a bathrobe — not the most dignified outfit to confront Sheriff Clayhorn in. At the very least you'd require your own pair of cowboy boots just to be able to look him in the chin. I was bare-footed. When I thought about it, I realised that of the three of us, I was the one who looked like an escaped convict or a refugee from a mental hospital.

The deputy introduced himself as Clyde Barrow and claimed kinship with a famous outlaw of the same name in the Depression era. I was around in those days but not in Texas. I'd heard of him vaguely, but I was in Chicago at the time and we weren't too impressed by backwoods bankrobbers. Apparently he was very famous in Texas, having the important credential of being born there.[43] Deputy Barrow, it turned out, wanted to talk movies.

He steered the big county Buick with one casual hand

Evidently not wanting to look like a hick, he'd dispensed with the chewing tobacco and puffed on a small cigar as he drove. 'You an actor, Mr Kelly?'

'I have been. Not so much lately. Getting a bit old for it.' I didn't know which way the conversation would turn, and I didn't think it would hurt to apply for a little sympathy.

'Now that's a business I really would like to get into. I reckon I could do pretty good at it and you know the part I'd really admire to play?'

'No.'

'Clyde Barrow of course. My cousin. Now he had a life to make a movie of. A real mean man, but with a good streak, you understand what I'm sayin'? Never stole from poor folks at all.'

What would be the point? I thought, but I let him rattle on.

PETER CORRIS

'Yes, sir, quite a time ol' Clyde had along with that Bonnie Parker. Good lookin' woman, mighty good-lookin', and smart too. Why, d'you know she wrote poetry about her and Clyde?'

I showed a polite interest I didn't in the least feel. Bad mistake of course — if this Clyde was really some kind of kin to the outlaw, who had only been dead for twenty years or so, he might have had rights to the property which I could have bought up and made a million from.[44] My life has been peppered with these sorts of missed opportunities. The only consolations are, you don't know you're missing them at the time and a lot of other people are in the same boat.

'I shore would like Elizabeth Taylor to play Bonnie,' Deputy Barrow said.

Such is the stuff that Hollywood dreams are made of. Here was this tobacco-chewing hillbilly dreaming of playing opposite Liz in a picture about a small-time holdup merchant whose girlfriend apparently wrote doggerel. It was too sad to laugh at and I just nodded and muttered something about talking to somebody about it.

'Would you, Mr Kelly? Would you really do that? I'd shore appreciate it.'

How many times have I and others made that promise and how rarely is it ever honoured? Certainly this time I forgot about it almost immediately because we'd pulled up outside the sheriff s office and it was time for me to run the gauntlet of curious onlookers in my bare feet, dirty shirt and bathrobe. Thank god there were no photographers present — this was not an image I wanted preserved for posterity. Clyde threw away his cigar end and was once again the tough law officer, escorting me from the car a little more roughly than was needed.

We were herded into Clayhorn's office. The sheriff lifted his legs from the desk, unfolded himself and stretched up in a massive jaw-cracking yawn. His big hands almost touched the ceiling. 'Well, well, what have we got here? Mr Cortez and Mr Kelly, the gun-toting bodyguards. Plus Presido County's leading drunk citizen. Howdy, Duane.'

'Howdy, sheriff. You think I might lie down in a cell for a time? There's going to be a power of talkin' and I'm disinclined to it.'

Clayhorn waved a magnanimous hand. 'You know where they are Duane. Go to it.'

Tardbetter shuffled off. The deputies exchanged looks and Barrow seemed to be appointed spokesman without a word being said. Pedro and I sat down while the deputy stood at semi-attention, awaiting permission to speak.

'You get on back to work Billy-Lee,' the sheriff said. 'Let's hear it, Clyde. No cussing and keep it short.'

Barrow launched into an account of the incident that was more or less accurate and included Pedro's accusation that Duane Tardbetter had attempted to murder me, had shot at Mr James Dean earlier and had written some threatening letters. Clayhorn didn't take notes or seem very interested. He doodled with a pencil on the back of a wanted poster while Barrow was speaking, nodded when he'd finished and told the deputy to return to work. Barrow had done his best to put me in a good and sympathetic light and he shot me a look before he left. I gave him a wink.

The sheriff threw down his pencil and leaned forward towards us across his desk. His lantern-jawed face lost its sleepy look and took on a frightening intensity. 'That's the biggest load of horseshit I ever heard. Duane Tardbetter can't write. In fact Sara-May's the only Tardbetter I ever heard of learned to write, leading me to think that she ain't really a Tardbetter after all, which wouldn't surprise anybody as knew her momma.'

Pedro looked worried. 'Sheriff, I...'

'Shut up! I've done a little checking on you since we had our first talk and what I hear leads me to believe you're a troublemaker. Now, you can swear out a complaint against Duane, get me involved in a lot of paperwork and court procedure which tires my patience more than some, or you can just stand up and walk outa here, leaving that pistol licence on my desk. Which is it to be?'

Pedro never was a fool. Mustering all the dignity he could, he stood, took out his wallet and removed a slip of folded paper which he put on the desk. He gave me a nod which was impossible to interpret and walked out of the office, closing the door quietly behind him.

'Smart man,' Clayhorn said. He looked at me as if seeing my unorthodox outfit for the first time. With features as craggy as his it was hard to tell, but I thought he might actually have been smiling.

'I'm sure you're a smart man too,' he said. 'Although a body wouldn't know it to look at you now. You just sit where you are and... '

I didn't like that smile and it's never a good idea to let someone do all the talking. I pointed to my strapped up ankle. 'Can't do anything else, sheriff. I'm practically a cripple.'

'That's a shame, Mr Browning, a terrible shame. Just let me make a phone call. There's a couple of fellers come into town all anxious to meet you.'

CHAPTER TWENTY-TWO

DARK suits, pork pie hats, pale faces, weekly barbering, peas in a pod. What else could they have been but G-men? When they walked into Hud Clayhorn's office I knew I'd been double-crossed by the lawyer Brennan. It didn't surprise me but I still cursed myself for trusting one of that species. Trust a lawyer and you can be almost certain that, whatever your problem was, it will get worse. The slightly older-looking of the two, and neither of them had hit thirty, plonked some papers down on the sheriffs desk.

'Any charges pending against this man, sheriff?' he said in a tone that meant he knew the answer.

'No, sir, Mr Burgess.' Clayhorn was mocking the man but in a way he couldn't object to.

'Then we can take him off your hands.' Burgess produced a pair of handcuffs from the slim attaché case he was carrying. He handed them to the other man. 'Cuff him, Mr McAlpine.'

'I protest!' I tried to stand but the ankle wouldn't let me and I sank back onto the hard chair, jarring my spine. 'I claim a citizen's right to...'

'You ain't no citizen of Texas, mister,' the sheriff said. 'You may or may not be a citizen of the United States. From what I'm hearin' there's room for argument on that point. Either way, these here Federal officers are the men to take you in charge.'

'I'm crippled,' I said. 'I can't walk.'

'We get a few like that,' Clayhorn said. 'I figure to help out whenever I can. Doc Clanton's been mighty helpful passing on equipment to me.' He got up and opened a broom cupboard beside the gun rack. There were a few crutches sitting beside a broom, a spade and an axe. He measured me with his eyes and selected one. 'This'd 'bout fit you I reckon.'

McAlpine put the handcuffs on and lifted me up, tucking the crutch under my shoulder. 'Let's go, Mr Browning,' he said.

The pair of them marched me out the door, Burgess giving the sheriff a nod of thanks. Clayhorn saluted him, still mocking but obviously glad to be rid of me. A dark blue Packard was parked outside the office. McAlpine opened the back door, whipped away the crutch and shoved me inside. Burgess settled in beside me and McAlpine got in behind the wheel.

'Where are we going?' I said.

'Best thing for you to do is shut up for a while and listen.' Burgess unbuttoned his jacket and let me see the holstered pistol in his armpit, always a convincing demonstration. McAlpine started the car and drove sedately around the corner, into Main Street and then took a turn onto the road that led away from the residential area and into the desert. After a few minutes we were clear of shops and houses and passing by the few small holdings on the fringe of the town. We left those behind and got out into the flat, dry country that stretched away to Mexico, travelling west towards the sun which was blazing at us out of a clear blue sky. McAlpine put on dark glasses. I closed my eyes.

There had been a few solid jolts of whisky in the flask and I was still feeling its effects, a mixture of despair and false courage. The crutch was lying across my legs. For one mad moment I thought of picking it up, bashing Burgess and using it to break McAlpine's neck from behind. Ridiculous. Burgess was staring out the window, looking half asleep, but he was more than twenty years younger than me and I had no doubt he could have that gun out before I got a good grip on the crutch. My ankle was throbbing and I could feel the crusted blood around my ear. The whisky courage was ebbing very rapidly.

'I need a smoke,' I said. 'Got any cigarettes?'

Burgess fished out a pack of Luckies and let me take one with my manacled hands. He took one himself and lit us up, his first humane act towards me. I tried to feel encouraged, but they let a condemned man have a last smoke, don't they?

'Thanks,' I said. 'I'm ready to start listening like you said, but I don't hear any talking.'

Burgess cranked his window down and blew smoke out. There was an ashtray mounted on the back of the front seat and he opened it. He reached across, took my cigarette and crushed it out.

'Hey...'

'Be respectful, Browning. When the time comes, you'll be talked to and you'll listen. Meantime, be respectful and don't crack wise. I don't like it.'

A statement like that is irresistible to someone like me, especially as I was now feeling a little more hopeful. You don't talk seriously to someone you plan to kill, do you? 'What happened to the "Mr"? And what makes you think my name's Browning? It's Kelly. You can see it for yourself on my driver's licence and other things if you weren't so keen on driving to Chihuahua.'

Burgess ignored me and we drove on for a few minutes before he reached forward and tapped McAlpine on the shoulder. 'This is it. Turn off here.'

Here was nothing to my mind. Just a point on the road with uneven, rocky ground on either side and barely a blade of grass showing. Then, as McAlpine slowed and made the turn to the right, I noticed a large rock that seemed somehow out of place — a marker, recently positioned. I looked ahead over McAlpine's shoulder and saw that we were following a track that hadn't had much traffic in recent times, say, for the past twenty years, but still showed signs of wheel ruts and flattening. It ran slightly uphill towards a mound where a couple of water-starved, wind-whipped cottonwoods struggled for existence.

Jesus Christ, I thought, and my hopeful feelings evaporated. Maybe you talk seriously before you act seriously. *They're going to lynch me!*

The car stopped in the meagre shade provided by the trees and the two FBI men got out and began smartening themselves up. They each combed their short hair, using the car's side mirror, straightened their ties and brushed down their suits. Both had removed their hats during the drive. Now they inspected them for dust, wiped the sweatbands with clean handkerchiefs and replaced them carefully on their heads. Burgess took out a pen knife and carefully cleaned his fingernails. McAlpine inspected his hands and evidently found them satisfactory. Both men then lit cigarettes and gazed towards the east, like a couple of Arabs waiting for prayer time.

I sat in the car, sweltering and fearful, but reluctant to say or do anything. At least they weren't fetching rope and shovels from the trunk. I discovered a box of matches in the pocket of my bathrobe and I picked the long butt out of the ashtray and lit it. A little piece of defiance, just to show that I hadn't completely knuckled under. Burgess and McAlpine continued to look east and I wriggled across the seat and looked out the open door in the same direction. I could see a few birds wheeling about and some clouds — a typical Texas landscape, which is to say, empty.

I heard the helicopter before I saw it, the way you do. A drone in the distance, then a dot appears and begins to take shape as the noise grows louder. You didn't see helicopters flying around every day of the week in those days the way you do now, and there was still something frighteningly futuristic-looking about them. The FBI men dropped their cigarettes, stamped them out and went through their clothes straightening drill again. Burgess whipped around and saw me leaning out of the car about to take a drag on the Lucky.

'Put that out!' he snapped.

I took the drag and flicked the butt at him. It hit his trouser leg and he jumped as if he'd been shot. The chopper was getting closer and Burgess was getting red in the face. He looked as if he wanted to shoot me. Instead, he stood on the smouldering butt and hastily brushed his pants down. Then he imitated his colleague by throwing his shoulders back and tucking in his chin, standing almost to attention, as the helicopter touched down about thirty yards away.

The chopper blades threw up dust and grit that made a mess of the G-men's careful grooming. They ignored it and continued to hold their poses. The blades stopped and the door of the helicopter opened. Two men climbed down, one a tall, loose-limbed type who seemed to blend in with the landscape despite his pilot's overalls, and the other a short, dapper character who held his hat in his hand and caressed his hair before putting the hat in place. He looked at the ground as he walked with short, hesitant steps, as if unsure what this rough, dirty stuff beneath his feet was. He was sallow-skinned and thick-waisted, middle-aged and out of condition. When he was ten yards away I recognised him from the set of his fleshy jaw and the suspicious and mistrustful look of his dark, hooded eyes — J. Edgar Hoover, the FBI *supremo*.

I haven't had a lot to do with famous people in my time, apart from movie stars who don't really count. They're famous, but not important, if you know what I mean. Sports people are much the same — I knew Les Darcy quite well when I was young and once played tennis against 'Big' Bill Tilden.[45] I chauffeured Sir Arthur Conan Doyle in London after the Great War and I suppose you have to count Howard Hughes as famous,[46] although stark staring mad is what he basically was. I suppose Edgar Hoover was the most powerful man I ever met and, even though he's been dead for around ten years, I still hesitate to speak candidly about him.[47]

PETER CORRIS

He approached the two agents and gave them a nod. 'Good work, boys. It'll go on your files.'

Files, as everyone knows, were sacred to J. Edgar. Burgess and McAlpine seemed to grow a couple of inches, watered by praise. Burgess sprang to open the trunk of the Packard. He lifted out a folding camp stool, dusted the seat and placed it on the ground. Hoover sat, only a couple of feet away from me now, and condescended to look in my direction. His hooded, brooding stare was enough to make you lose your lunch, if you'd had any. He waved his hand imperiously and the two agents, along with the pilot moved away out of earshot.

'Richard Kelly Browning,' Hoover said in a soft voice that carried a trace of southern accent. 'Born Noo-castle, Australia, fifty-nine years of age. Served in Australian army in World War I. Rank, private, no decorations, no record of discharge. Entered USA illegally 1919 from Mexico. Arrested for gun-running in Canada in 1920 and entered USA, again illegally, from Canada in that year. Pilot and movie actor, declared bankrupt 1930, granted US citizenship 1938 for services rendered to FBI. Private Investigator, California, 1943–4. Honorary rank US military 1944–5. Proprietor Sherman House, dramatic academy, Sherman Oaks, California.'

In fact the FBI had reneged on the deal to grant me US citizenship after I'd helped them bust up the Ku Klux Klan in Hollywood in 1938, and only came through four years later when I'd been of further service.[48] Otherwise, it was pretty accurate, although it left out my military service in Mexico and Canada along with a few other things less meritorious. All in all, as I calculated it, there was about as much to be proud of as to be ashamed about. I stuck my hands out.

'Pretty impressive, huh? I'm glad to meet you, Mr Hoover.'

He ignored my hands, and when he looked at me it was as if he was looking at something that belonged under a rock. 'Impressive isn't the word I'd use. I've never seen a record so full of holes and

150

ah, ambiguities. It offends my sense of... completeness. You're a bad egg, Mr Browning, a rotten apple.'

'I helped you twice,' I protested. 'Those guys in the bedsheets were going to assassinate every rich Jew in Hollywood and...'

'That's an exaggeration.' As he said this I got the feeling Hoover thought the plan wasn't such a bad idea. 'And the only reason you helped was that we'd have slung your ass out of the country if you hadn't. Am I right?'

He was and he wasn't, but he wasn't looking to debate the matter. Hoover, as I discovered over the next few minutes, was as full of acting tricks as James Dean. He could switch from down-homey to hard-ass bureaucrat in a split second and his doubling-up of the metaphors and throwing in of rhetorical questions was all a technique to get the upper hand. He didn't have to work very hard to get it with me — here he was in his five hundred dollar suit with three armed off-siders while I was unshaven, half-naked, half-crippled and smelling like a polecat.

I nodded sullenly. 'Whatever you say.'

'Now *that's* getting something to be like the right attitude. A mite reluctant maybe but getting there.'

'You're holding all the cards, Mr Hoover. What do you want from me?'

He looked me over carefully before answering, taking in my battered and dilapidated appearance. He knew I didn't have any influence to wield, and from the way his eyes glittered I could tell he was enjoying this moment of total power. I looked up at the nearest horizontal branch on the straggling cottonwood. I didn't think the FBI men were going to lynch me — I had a feeling it would be something worse.

I was so nervous my legs shook and the matchbox in the pocket of my robe started to jiggle. I was sweating and parched and I sensed that the fastidious Hoover would have liked there to be more distance between us. He adopted another course by taking out his cigar case, flicking it open and offering me a long panatella.

'I only smoke after meals myself,' he said. 'Not my choice —
doctor's orders. But perhaps you'd care to indulge now?'

I took a cigar and lit it. Cuban. Delicious. This was a few years
before Castro made the smoking of Havanas un-American. I resolved
to myself never to smoke anything else if I got out of this fix and it's
one resolution I've more or less kept.

'Thank you.' I blew the smoke over the top of Hoover's immac-
ulate hat.

'Mr Browning, I get the sense that you're a person who hasn't
fulfilled his potential. I'm about to change all that.'

The smoke suddenly tasted less sweet. 'What d'you mean?'

'You're about to become known as the man who rid the world
of Lucky Luciano.'

CHAPTER TWENTY-THREE

ACCORDING to Hoover, Luciano was still in Mexico and arrangements had been made to keep him there, permanently. Someone had to be the patsy and I was the perfect candidate — last seen driving Charley Lucky to Mexico, radical change in appearance, change of identity, no record of re-entering the United States. The FBI undertook to consolidate my new identity, re-locate me and set me up in some kind of business. Nothing about the idea appealed to me, but Hoover's manner indicated that I didn't have much choice. Again I got the feeling that there might be more dangerous instruments in the trunk of the Packard than a camp stool.

'People *know* I'm back in the States,' I said. 'James Dean, Brennan, Pedro Cortez, Sheriff Clayhorn... '

'That can all be taken care of,' Hoover said.

'What about my wife?'

'What about her? I understand she doesn't know where you are. All you have to do is play a waiting game, Dick. Bide your time and you can get together with her again. I'm a great believer in the family. Why, the two of you might meet up again in Australia. How about that? That'd sure be nice.'

'Bide my time?'

'Sure. Lie low for, say, six months while everything slots into place. It's going to take a power of organising. We'll look after you.'

The cigar wasn't tasting good at all by this time but I kept smoking it. I'd have smoked it if it had tasted like rubber and I'd have drunk battery fluid. I was in a desperate spot and I knew it. I *had* to agree. Here I was talking to a man who was setting about arranging an assassination with all the trimmings. As I pondered I recalled the rumours that had been running around for years that the guy Hoover, his agents and the cops nailed outside the Biograph wasn't John Dillinger but some poor unfortunate lookalike. A patsy, in other words.[49] I was in the hands of experts and I had to risk everything on one question. I took a long drag on the cigar and expelled the smoke slowly.

'I can't see why you need me to agree to this. Why not just bump me now and set it up anyway you like? You'll understand my concern.'

Hoover laughed, actually laughed. He was in his element, enjoying every moment of it. 'I'm really just a policeman, Mr... Kelly. Sworn to uphold the law at all times. My methods might get a little unorthodox now and then. I might get a little...creative, but I'm downright insulted by your suggestion that I'd be a party to your murder.'

'I'm sorry.'

'Besides, we need things from you — some telephone calls, certain documents, like letters. Photographs maybe, fingerprints on selected items. You understand me?'

I dropped the cigar end out onto the rough ground between the stool and the car and watched it smoulder for a second or two before I nodded. 'Ok, Mr Hoover. I'll do what you ask, but I'm giving up an old life and taking an enormous risk with the new one and there'll have to be a considerable...financial inducement at some point in the proceedings.'

Hoover smiled. 'I hoped you'd say something like that. I think you understand things perfectly. Congratulations, you just saved your miserable, worthless life.'

That was it. He got up off his stool, nodded to Burgess and McAlpine and went back with his pilot to the helicopter. A few minutes later and he was just part of a droning dot, heading towards the horizon.

'Nice guy,' I said to the agents. 'Gave me a cigar. I didn't notice him give you two a cigar. Why would that be?'

'Don't get cute,' Burgess said. 'I still don't like you.'

'Ah, but you've gotta be nice to me, don't you? That makes a difference. Now let's see, I sure could do with a drink, and a bath and a change of clothes. A good meal wouldn't go amiss either and... What the hell are you doing?'

From the trunk McAlpine took out my suitcase and a few other personal items, like my boots, cowboy hat and pistol harness. He opened the case and removed the bag I kept my shaving tackle in. Then he put an enamel dish on the seat his boss had occupied and filled it with water from a large jerry can. A cake of soap and a towel also appeared.

'Get cleaned up, Mr Kelly. You're going on a little trip.' He unlocked the handcuffs.

Burgess examined the .38, checking it for weight and balance. He wheeled, dropped into a crouch and fired six rounds into the trunk of a tree about thirty feet away. Rapid fire. Good pattern. Birds that had been disturbed by the chopper had settled back into the trees. Now they flew up into the sky again, squawking and calling.

'Nice weapon,' the agent said. 'I'll be sure to take real good care of it for you.'

I shrugged as I climbed out of the car and used the crutch to hobble across to the bowl. 'Have you got any water for drinking?'

'Better than that.' McAlpine hauled out a bottle of Wild Turkey bourbon and one of those plastic cups that concertina down. Then he produced a lunchbox of the kind factory and construction workers carry, opened it and took out some sandwiches wrapped in wax paper. 'Everything you need.'

'How about some coffee to finish up?'

McAlpine took a thermos flask from the trunk and held it high. 'Get cleaned up and get dressed if you want some of these comforts,' he said. 'And don't piss against the wheel of the car.'

I wanted the comforts very badly and I did the best I could under the circumstances. The water in the bowl was warm and I managed a rough shave, cleaning up around the edges of my neat beard. I washed and pulled on a clean shirt and underwear. There was no way I could get my strapped-up foot into a pair of pants, but Burgess obliged me by using his pen knife to slit the leg of my jeans. I ended up halfway respectable with everything vital covered, wearing my socks and one boot.

This rough toilet refreshed me considerably and I swung over to Doc Clanton's optimistic view that I'd probably survive uncrippled. Burgess and McAlpine smoked and discussed FBI things among themselves. I completed my ablutions by hobbling across to the tree Burgess had shot at and pissing long and hard against it.

'I'm ready for that drink now. Going to join me boys?'

They declined, but we shared the sandwiches and they drank some coffee while I took a few solid jolts of the Wild Turkey with warmish water. The ankle was still hurting and I accepted a couple of aspirin tablets from McAlpine. I decided they were pretty nice fellows, for G-men, that is. I was feeling pretty mellow by now, what with the sun low on the horizon and all, and I suggested that it was about time we got back to Marfa.

'You c'n watch them makin' the picture,' I said. 'Nearly finished. Get to meet 'Lizabeth Taylor and James Dean. How'd you like that? Get to meet Rock Hudson himself.'

'That'd be fine, Mr Kelly,' Burgess said. 'Agent McAlpine and I'd certainly enjoy that.

Why don't you get in the car now and we can move along.'

'Right,' I said. 'In the car. Bloody ankle's still sore.'

'You sounded like an Englishman just then,' McAlpine said.

They helped me to the back seat and I more or less crawled in and lay along the length of it. 'Australian,' I muttered. 'Greatest country on earth, Australia. Greatest climate, best beaches, best tennis players. Lew Hoad, greatest player of all time except...' I remember saying this but I know I didn't complete the thought and I never have.[50] I still wonder what I meant.

CHAPTER TWENTY-FOUR

'Forward, 185!'

I was supposed to shove the bucket and mop out of the cell with my foot, step over it and present myself and the cell for inspection. I was in D wing of the military section of the Federal penitentiary at Leavenworth, Kansas. 185 were the last three digits of my number, the rest of which I forget. Prisoners in D wing had a cell each and were allowed a few comforts, such as a radio for two hours per day, a weekly hot shower and unlimited borrowing from the prison library, but we received no visitors and were not permitted to speak unless requested to by a guard. It was not quite solitary confinement in that we could see our fellow inmates at cell-inspection time, exercise hour and at church, but the rule of silence made it worse than solitary in some ways.

I recalled nothing of the drive from Texas and had woken up in the cell, dressed in prison denims, shaved and crop-headed. A piece of paper was pinned to my chest on which the regulations governing D division were printed. The statement about silence was heavily underlined and I got the message. I was in a kind of limbo. I had no idea what paperwork there was on me in the prison, if any. I didn't know what my offence or sentence were supposed to be. The silence rule was enforced with the very compelling argument of the billy club and a sensible man didn't challenge it.

Otherwise, the discipline wasn't so harsh. I'd experienced worse in Long Bay and other places. The guards were the usual brutal thugs, the doctors the usual brain-dead alcoholics and the chaplains were away with the fairies of their various persuasions. In some ways the semi-isolation was a blessing; I didn't have to worry about the predatory homosexuals who were the scourge of life in general prisons, nor informers or stir-crazy escape-plotters. The boredom and the empty hours were the main torment, along with the uncertainty of my situation. The routine, and that's what prison life consists of above all, was: lights on and a wake-up bell at six a.m.; wash and shave (beards were forbidden and a razor was issued and re-claimed each morning); cell clean-up and inspection; breakfast eaten in the cell; two hours of nothing; two hours of work; lunch in the cell; two more blank hours; one hour of exercise before being locked back in the cell at four p.m. where we stayed for the evening meal and the next eighteen hours. The food was bland and starchy, but bearable. The coffee was thin and adulterated with chicory. The tobacco ration consisted of two plugs per week of rock-hard stuff that had to be shaved with a thumbnail and rubbed hard before it would light. The issued cigarette papers were thin and too lightly gummed. The two hours of radio came through in this period, not always at the same time. We had no control over the program which was mostly music I didn't like and commercials for things I didn't want. No news broadcasts.

The work details didn't offer a lot of stimulation — painting a part of the penitentiary that was undergoing renovation, stints in the prison laundry, licence plate stamping and yard sweeping. I was never much of a reader and the stuff in the library didn't interest me — the trolley that came around held mostly law books and westerns and it's pretty hard to pick a good book just by pointing to the title on the spine, which was all we were allowed to do. The only thing to be said for having a good few years on the clock, and it only really applies I imagine to prison sentences and long sea voyages, is that empty time passes more quickly than it did when you were young.

As an old institutional hand, I had an almost instinctual knowledge of the way to loosen up the bonds of a rigid system.

Malingering is far and away the best method. When I felt I couldn't stand the boredom and routine any longer, I deliberately cut down on my food intake and hoarded my tobacco for a smoking binge. My appetite was poor anyway (I've never been very interested in food except as a blotter for booze) and I'd lost weight since entering the prison. A week of starvation, heavy smoking and pacing my cell at night induced a fever, a few tremors and various other symptoms it wasn't difficult to exaggerate.

I began this account of my time in Leavenworth with a guard's order to move forward. For forty-nine days — according to the tally I'd kept with spent matches — I'd obeyed, but not this morning. I lay on my bunk feeling genuinely feverish and weak, very prepared to accept proper medication and nursing. The guard rapped on the bars with his club.

'Forward!'

No response from Browning, or Kelly or whoever the hell I was supposed to be. The guard slammed the door shut and I was left in peace. I had no idea what the procedure was in this place but I felt myself equal to the occasion. After a couple of hours the door slid back and one of the piss-pot doctors put his head into the cell. I'd heard him coming and had held my breath for as long as I could manage, thus achieving a fast pulse rate and heightened blood pressure. I needn't have bothered, he wasn't going to be that thorough.

'What's the matter with you?' the doctor asked from just inside the doorway. He was hanging there as if afraid the door would shut on him.

'He's on silence, doc,' the guard immediately behind him said. 'Probably won't answer you.'

'How am I going to tell what's wrong with him?'

The guard elbowed the doctor aside. 'I'll check him out. What do I look for?'

The guard approached my bunk, bent over me and I took a slow, gentle swing at him with my right fist. The punch landed on his flabby jaw with all the force of a snowflake. The guard chuckled throatily and scarcely moved.

'Hell,' he said. 'This guy's as weak as a fucking kitten. Don't reckon I'd even have to report that as an attempted assault.'

Nevertheless, the doctor had retreated towards the door. 'What colour is he?'

'Shit, doc, he's a white man. Ain't no niggers in here.'

'I mean is he pale, flushed or what?' The guard leaned down. In fact I was strong enough to flatten his nose and remove some teeth and I was sorely tempted, but I lay still. 'Both, seems to me. Yep, I'd say he was pale *and* flushed. What's that mean?'

'Sick bay,' the saintly doctor said.

It's a strange fact, but in my experience prison hospitals are usually a lot better than you'd expect given the unpleasantness of the places they serve. It's as if the planners feel a bit guilty about the general awfulness and build in at least one humane element. I've been told that the hospitals in some of the high-class minimum security facilities rival the Mayo Clinic and I can believe it, although I hope never to find out personally. The Leavenworth hospital wasn't too bad. I was in a ward with six other men — genuinely very ill fellows — and the no-talking rule wasn't in force. That was the first great improvement. The second was that the penitentiary's bootleg liquor network took in the hospital, unlike D wing. The food was the same, the tobacco was the same but we got an extra hour of radio per day.

Of course the great advantage was being treated, not exactly like a human being, but at least as a medical case, which might not sound like much, but it's a hell of a lot better than just being a number. There was the interest of the doctor's examinations and the attentions of the ward nurses and orderlies — male of course, you can't have everything. The security was tight — barred windows, guards on the doors and no useful implements left lying about.

From the window of my cell in D wing I could see the exercise yard; from the window in the ward I could see an internal road, a couple of administration buildings and some small garden plots along with a few patches of lawn. I'm no great nature lover, but those bits of greenery did me a lot of good.

One of the first requirements was the compilation of 185's medical history. I was subjected to a thorough physical which involved inspection of all protuberances and orifices and was pronounced clear of venereal disease. Then I sat down with a youngish doctor, not yet reduced to a drunkard by the system, to be grilled about my illnesses from day one. I found it amazingly enjoyable. To be forbidden to talk for several weeks and then to be invited to talk as much as you liked and all about yourself was like being given the key to the candy store. I resolved not to disappoint the doctor.

'A sickly child?' he queried.

I nodded. 'Very. Not expected to survive a week — underweight, difficulty in breathing, bad colour. My parents had lost five before me and pretty much gave me up. But I pulled through, as you see.'

'Yes. Do you know why?'

'Sure. The Aborigines.'

'Excuse me?'

'I was born in the Australian bush. My father despaired at the thought of losing yet another son and he took to me the local black medicine man. The *ngalanana*, as they call them. He smoked me, rubbed me with goanna oil and kangaroo blood and I came through.'

He was scribbling fast. 'Remarkable.'

'Right. I was as strong as a lion as a kid — great athlete, swimmer, all that. I wrestled a shark in Botany Bay once. Got a few scratches but we ended up eating the shark.'

'Australians eat sharks?'

'All the time.' That was about the first truthful thing I told him.[51] I rattled on like this for a while, inventing furiously because in truth I'd scarcely had a day's illness in my life. Broken bones and bullet wounds, yes, but not much else. Except tuberculosis. I'd had a bout of that more than twenty years back after I'd spent an unfortunate time as a hobo, my lowest ebb.[52] This was getting into tricky territory and I wondered how to play it — it could give me a ticket out into a sanitarium maybe if I could convince them I'd had a recurrence. Even a prolonged stay in these relatively pleasant surroundings would be something. On the other hand, they might just lose interest in me as someone who was on the way out. Back in the 30s the only treatment was fresh air, rest and hope — plus prayer if you were that way inclined. It had worked for me. I'd heard that they had new drugs for the disease nowadays,[53] maybe it wasn't taken so seriously. I decided to risk it.

'Tuberculosis,' I said in answer to his question about serious illnesses in adulthood.

He checked the file he had on me and nodded. 'Yes, I see. Hmm. Give me the details.'

Of course I spun him a tale about contracting the disease while working on banana boats between Honduras and Los Angeles. I laid it on thick, talking about the incredibly hard work, the appalling conditions, bad diet and reliance on rum to keep going.

'Why were you doing work like that? You're an educated man?'

Time to plant a seed. 'Well, doctor, it was kind of...undercover work. I can't say anymore about it.'

He jotted down everything I said and then referred to my file again. 'You're very underweight for a man of your height and build. I think we should run some tests to see if the tuberculosis has come back.'

I contrived to look terrified. 'God, don't say that. They told me it'd kill me for sure if it came back.'

The doctor laughed. 'Back then it might have, but things have moved on since then. Where did you get this medical advice, in Honduras or LA?'

I had to consider that one and the germ of an idea was forming. 'I believe I was in Montana when the diagnosis was made. I went to work on a cattle ranch and the clean air cured me.'

'It'd be a help to have those medical records. Where are they?'

This was the opportunity I'd been hoping for. I furrowed my brow. 'It's a long time ago and I've moved around a good deal. I'm not sure.'

'Who was your physician?'

Firm ground. 'Old "Spot" Barclay. A great guy, but he's long dead, god rest his soul.' This doctor had a slightly preachy look to him, so I threw that in for good measure and it didn't seem to do any harm. 'My wife might be able to find them,' I went on, 'if I could get a message to her...'

'That might be possible. I'll see what I can do. Meantime, 185, back to the ward with you for a rest and we'll start the tests tomorrow.'

'The tests, what do they consist of?'

'Oh, just taking some blood samples for a start. Nothing too drastic. We'll know the result inside a week.'

Not a bad start. 'And if it is there, what then?'

He clapped me on the shoulder and I allowed myself to rock back a little although he was a weedy little type I could've snapped in two. 'We can handle it. Clear it up in no time in a man with a constitution like yours. Don't worry.'

'Thanks, doctor.'

I was escorted back to the ward and made sure to move slowly and take frequent rests. Back when I had TB I remember that shortness of breath and physical weakness were part of the problem.

The guard wasn't sympathetic. 'Bad news?'

'Maybe.'

'Tough. One of the guys in your ward died this morning. You could be next.'

I ignored that and moved even more slowly until he was hissing with impatience.

Back in the ward the atmosphere was gloomy. There were two unoccupied beds — mine and the one immediately opposite. Joe 'Knuckleball' Faulkner. He was a lifer in the true sense of the word — sentenced in the late 1920s when he was a few days short of his twenty-first birthday for the murder of a policeman, he'd served over thirty years and must have played thousands of games of prison baseball — hence his nickname. He'd chewed tobacco incessantly the whole of the time he was inside and the cancer ate his throat out quickly and then took its time about the rest of him. The other men were a collection of long-term prisoners, a couple of them soldiers, serving time for crimes of violence. One had heart trouble, one had cancer and the other complaints I forget.

'Hey, Dick,' the other cancer sufferer said, striving hard to be tough and buoyant, 'you playing in the big league now?'

I was going by the name of Dick Kelly and had told them I was in for shooting an officer. It seemed to be something they could all understand. I shrugged and lit a cigarette, equally tough. 'Could be. Lung trouble, maybe.'

'Naw, they can fix that shit. Let's play cards. Winner buys some juju juice for a toast to the old 'Knuckleball'.'

The next day I was given a pen and paper and instructed to write to my wife asking her to find the medical records. She was to send them to a post office box in Kansas City. Tricky stuff. Louise, of course, wouldn't have the faintest idea of what I was talking about. That didn't worry me — all I wanted to do was tell her where I was and beg her to do something to get me out. But how?

'Any of you boys know anything about invisible ink?'

'Lemon juice,' one said.

I nodded. 'Yeah, I just happen to have a lemon here with me. Thanks.'

PETER CORRIS

The heart patient, a morose type focussed hard on his impend-
ing death, sat up in bed, momentarily interested. 'You got all you
need. Piss'll do it, providing it gets looked at in a couple of days in
a dry climate.'

I wrote a straightforward message to Louise asking her to look
for the records of my treatment for tuberculosis in Montana in 1935
and asking her to forward them to the address designated. I said I
was well and hoped to see her soon. No further explanations as per
orders. I pissed into a cup, sharpened a match and wrote as thickly
as I could at the bottom of the page:

Louise — I am in Leavenworth prison. Tell Bobby Silk he'll made a
million out of the story if he can get me out. Relying on you, all my
love, Dick.

The words disappeared and I handed the paper and pen over to
the guard. It felt like sealing a message in a bottle and chucking it
into the sea. I wonder if that has ever worked?

They took some blood and ran their tests. I continued not to
eat and to smoke as much as I could. I felt sick all right — sick
with hope that alternated with despair. The doctor told me that the
tests were 'ambiguous' and would have to be done again. Ok by me,
although the company in the ward was beginning to get me down.
A few days later a guard opened the door and beckoned me forward.
I threw down my cards and shuffled over in my slippers and pyjamas. I realised I was becoming an invalid despite myself.

'More tests?'

He looked at me with distaste. 'Shave yourself and get your
clothes on. You've got a visitor.'

CHAPTER TWENTY-FIVE

'HI there, Dick. Nice try.'

The man waiting for me in the otherwise empty visiting room was FBI agent Burgess. Brown suit this time but otherwise everything just exactly as it should be. He had a slim briefcase on the desk in front of him and a packet of Chesterfield cigarettes. He wasn't smoking and he didn't get up to shake my hand. In fact he hardly moved at all. Disappointment flooded through me but I tried not to show it. I dropped into the chair opposite him and reached for the cigarettes. The guard stepped forward but Burgess gave him a nod and he pulled back. Another nod and he left the room. Burgess opened the briefcase and took out my letter to Louise.

'Like I say — nice try.'

I shrugged and lit the cigarette. After the prison-issue plug it tasted as if it had been cured in honey. My time on the silence wing came in handy — I decided to let Burgess do all the talking, at least at first.

'You reckon your story's worth a million? You're wrong. It isn't worth a plugged nickel.'

I shrugged again and went on smoking. He was here talking to me and that had to mean something.

'In fact, you haven't got a story. All you've got is a chance to stay alive by keeping your mouth shut.'

It was time to speak. 'I wouldn't call rotting in here being alive. You want to try it some time, Burgess. It'd be valuable experience for you.'

'You dumb ass. I'm not talking about Leavenworth. I'm talking about the outside. Being free.'

I glanced around to make sure the guard had closed the door. Then I looked under the table and overhead at the light. Burgess stared at me as if I'd gone mad, but I was looking for wires, microphones, tape machines.

'What the hell are you doing?'

I leaned closer to him, so close I could smell his shaving cologne and the oil he put on his hair. 'Has it happened then?' I whispered. 'We don't get to listen to the news in here and the only magazines I see are *Ring Illustrated* and *Hot Rods*.'

I wasn't looking forward to being, at however a long and protected remove, the man who killed Lucky Luciano, but I knew that if I stayed in the prison I'd die anyway of boredom or rotgut liquor.

Burgess put the letter carefully away in his briefcase and took out a newspaper. It was the *Washington Post* and it was open on the second page and folded to show the headline: LUCIANO ARRESTED IN SICILY. There was a photograph of Charley Lucky flanked by two Italian cops wearing big guns. Luciano didn't look too worried. Quite by accident, my eye dropped to another headline: BRITISH COMMANDOS TO FIGHT IN CYPRUS. At it again.

It might sound dumb, but I had trouble taking in the significance of the item about Luciano. I was overwhelmed by the fact of the newspaper itself. I wanted to grab it and read everything on every page, study every photograph, catch up on the football scores and see who was fighting who.

'I don't get it,' I said, reaching for another cigarette.

Burgess took one himself and lit it, leaving me to light my own. 'You're off the hook, Browning. Luciano got wind of what was in store for him and he got out of Mexico pronto. They picked him up in Italy, but that won't worry him none.'

I nodded. 'He doesn't look upset.'

'He owns more cops there than a dog has fleas.'

More even than he owns here, I was thinking. Someone had to have tipped him off. But it wasn't the moment to make the comment.

'So you don't need your patsy?'

'That's right. Now we've only got one little problem — this idea of yours to sell your story.'

'I was desperate,' I said. 'It was just something I said to get my agent fired up. He wouldn't help me unless he thought there was a buck in it.'

'We understand. Still, there's a worry in some circles. Pity we don't have that limey thing — the official secrets act. We could get you to sign that and shut you up forever.'

'I won't say anything. You have my word.'

I tried to say this with force and conviction which is hard to do when you're wearing prison denims, have your hair cut like a boot-camp rookie and haven't had a decent meal in weeks. Burgess snorted and took some more papers from his bag.

'I wouldn't piss on your word. To me, you're a bum and I'd plant you in a desert under a cactus if I was running things. But I'm not so here's what's going to happen. You're going to sign these papers.' He detached some sheets and thrust them at me. 'They're backdated and they induct you in the lowest possible rank in the Federal Bureau of Investigation. Then you sign these.' He hammered his fist on another set of forms. 'That discharges you as of now. With no pension or benefits I might add. As a former member of the FBI you're forbidden to publish anything relating to your service in the Bureau without express permission from the Director. Mr Hoover ain't likely to do that.'

'I suppose not. But this can't work. I'm bound to be asked questions about the Luciano thing, driving him to Mexico.'

Burgess shook his head. 'Case of mistaken identity. We got the cover-up all in place. It's old news already and if you deny everything the news hounds lose interest.'

'Why are you doing this for me.'

He sneered and laughed at the same time, not easy to do, but the effect is to leave you in no doubt about your worm status. 'None of it's for you. There's a bigger game which you don't know about and never will.'

'I agree to this and then I'm out?'

'As soon as they can process your ass through the system here. And Browning, the penalty for violation of this regulation is ten years in the Federal penitentiary. Guess where that time would most likely be spent?'

Burgess produced a pen from his jacket, uncapped it and handed it to me. I signed the first set of papers in three of four places marked with a cross. I put the pen down, looked at him and grinned. 'We're colleagues, Mr Burgess.'

'You're insulting me. Sign the others before I break your fuckin' nose.'

'Just one thing. I'm not leaving here with you. I didn't like that remark about the desert. I want independent transport.'

'I wouldn't walk you to the door, Browning. I'm out of here as soon as you sign. You'll get a bus ticket good for seventy-two hours to any state in the country.'

I signed and he gathered up the papers. 'Leave me the *Post*,' I said. 'I want to hear how Ike's hitting his long irons these days.'

He snatched the paper and tucked it away. 'You got no respect. I'm real sorry this plan didn't work. I reckon you'd have been feeding the fishes within days.'

'That's what I think, too,' I said.

I wasn't sure I was clear of the lime pit until I was escorted to the clearing room in the administration block — one of the places I could see from the hospital ward window. The grass and flower beds looked even better close up. I signed some more documents and was surprised to discover that I'd earned thirty-eight dollars and forty-three cents for the work I'd done in gaol. But Burgess and McAlpine had cleaned everything out of my room in Marfa, including my ready cash, amounting to more than six hundred dollars so I wasn't going to have to beg a meal on the outside. The only thing missing was the .38. Within an hour of suffering Burgess' last insult, I was dressed in my own clothes, which hung very loosely on my gaunt frame, and standing outside the prison waiting for a ride into town. I never heard any more about my blood tests.

It was a fine evening, I remember, but I wouldn't have cared if the rain had been coming down along with snow, sleet and a fifty mile an hour wind. A prison truck dropped me at the bus depot, but I did what every released convict who hasn't got religion or lost his mind while in the joint does first thing — I went straight to the nearest bar. The neon Budweiser sign flickering in the dying light was one of the prettiest things I'd ever seen, and the smell of beer, smoke and sweat was like French perfume after the disinfectant and stale air of the prison. I ordered a beer and double shot of whisky and drank them slowly, savouring every drop.

There was a glass-fronted case of cigars behind the bar and I bought six panatellas, lit up and began what has been nearly thirty years of devoted cigar smoking.

The bar was slowly filling up and getting noisy and I knew I should phone Louise before the din got too loud. But the first drinks had been so good. I ordered another shot and chaser. I felt the prison odour lifting off me and had an impulse to straighten my shoulders and stand tall. I realised that I'd been slumping more and more each day. A man standing next to me sniggered as I pulled myself erect.

'When you get out, buddy?'

I looked at him carefully. I was still thinking in prison terms — could this guy hurt me? Could I use him? He was middle-aged, balding, fat-gutted. A working stiff, construction maybe or a truck-driver. Harmless. I had a strong impulse to talk to someone, anyone.

'Just now.'

'How long you serve?'

'Not long but way too long.'

He nodded and looked down into his beer. The pink bald spot at the crown of his head made him seem innocent and vulnerable or even trustworthy, like a priest. I wanted to tell him all about it and had to take a long pull on the whisky to stop myself. *What if he was a plant, put right there to see if I could keep my mouth shut?*

He sighed. 'I was inside myself once. Sure was a bad time. I remember...'

But I'd downed my shot, stuck my cigar in my mouth and was moving away towards the phone holding my beer in a shaking hand. I was about to drop the dime when I had a sort of nightmare vision that the place was full of FBI men and that the barman — a stocky, bullet-headed character — was J. Edgar Hoover's brother. I had to get out of there. Probably it was just the effects of the rich cigar and potent liquor on a much-abused nervous system.

I used the ticket they'd given me to catch a Greyhound to Denver. Then it was over the Rockies and down to Las Vegas and on to LA, paying my own way. As best I could without getting thrown off as a pervert or madman, I inspected every person on that bus, suspecting a G-man's badge behind every lapel. Everyone, that is, except the coloured people sitting at the back. This was long before the FBI started recruiting blacks and Hispanics. Most of the passengers rushed off to gamble during the two-hour stopover in Las Vegas but not me. I still couldn't quite believe that I'd got out of the mess and that the FBI wasn't setting me up in some way. I went to a diner and ordered a big meal which I ate with nothing to drink but coffee. I wasn't taking any chances of letting my guard down while drunk. I sat with my back to a wall, jumped when the waitress brought the coffee, stared at everyone who came in and twitched when anyone looked at me. Of course, because I was behaving so strangely, plenty did.

I went through the same suspicious routine before the run to Los Angeles, moving around the bus, trying to detect undercover men. The fact that it was night and most of the passengers fell asleep almost straight away didn't help. I told myself I was on a path to the nuthouse if I kept this up and tried to settle my nerves by reading my way through the bunch of papers and magazines I'd bought at the bus station. There were riots in India and Argentina but the fighting had stopped in the Middle East. The German novelist, Thomas Mann, none of whose books I'd read, needless to say, had died at eighty. Good innings. The writing game seems to be good for longevity, which may be why I've taken it up, in a sense.[54]

Somehow this information comforted and reassured me. The world was still the same place, still crazy, a mixture of fun and fury. Nevertheless I nearly went through the roof as I felt a tap on my shoulder, just as I was drifting off to sleep.

'Mind if I have the sports page, bud?'

A man wearing a string tie and a ten gallon hat was bending over me, breathing bourbon fumes into my face. He smiled, showing a gold tooth.

'I see there's a story about Rocky fighting old Archie.[55] You a fight fan?'

'Yes, yes, sure I am,' I stammered. 'Yeah, take it. It's all yours.'

'Thanks, bud.'

I believed him. That natural and ordinary interest was all he wanted to satisfy. He was what he appeared to be, completely uninterested in me except as a guy who happened to have a newspaper. This simple exchange did me a lot of good and I fell asleep and stayed under until we rolled into LA on a clear, bright morning the way they used to be back then and haven't been for twenty years.

I strolled into the depot and went to a washroom to freshen up before calling Louise. What I saw in the mirror was a stranger — gaunt, crop-headed, pale-skinned, with a furtive, haunted look. Such hair as the prison barber had left was almost completely white as was my two-day beard. My teeth were stained yellow from the excessive smoking. In the three months since I'd left Hollywood I'd aged twenty years and I looked like an old man.

CHAPTER TWENTY-SIX

CAN'T let Louise see me like this. As Richard Kelly, I checked into a good hotel off Hollywood Boulevard and set about restoring the damage. I went to a dentist, had my teeth cleaned and some other restorative work done. Putting on a bit of condition was no problem — regular decent meals with plenty of beer, wine and bourbon would take care of that most agreeably. Los Angeles was definitely the place for male cosmeticising. A hairdressing establishment in Beverly Hills dyed and shaped my too-short but still thick hair and eyebrows, leaving a distinguished amount of grey at the temples. They gave me a manicure and a facial that helped to smooth away some of the effects of manual labour, poor diet and squinting in bad lights.

Clothes were the next priority. None of the stuff I'd worn in Texas fitted me or would do. I threw the lot away except the comfortable boots and bought a sports outfit and a suit, a couple of shirts, ties, three pairs of socks and shoes and two new hats. All this took about a week. The hotel had a swimming pool and I spent as much time in the sun as possible, re-acquiring the tan I was famous for. By the end of that time my funds were getting very low. Losing fifteen years and gaining ten pounds hadn't come cheap.

The jumpy feeling I'd had retreated little by little as the days went by and nothing scary happened. I kept clear of alleys, pool-halls and high bridges, but a prudent person does that anyway. I made a careful study of the trade papers to catch up with what had been happening in the dream factory while I was inside. The usual stuff. At Warners, they were shooting the interior scenes for *Giant;* at Fox they were making *Anastasia* with Ingrid Bergman and Helen Hayes; MGM were going hard on *High Society*, with Crosby, Sinatra and Kelly. Warners and George Stevens were going to have some pretty stiff competition. I was surprised to see that the advertisement I'd devised for Sherman House — with the girl on the horse and the guy springing from the diving board — wasn't running in *Variety*. I hoped Louise hadn't run into money trouble. With enough cash left to pay the hotel bill and not much more, I took a last check on my appearance. I was still thinner and older-looking than before, but at least I was recognisably Richard Browning. I put this to the test by walking up to a news-stand on Vine Street where I'd bought papers for years from Joey Knopfelmacher, a former jockey who'd given all his money to women, bookies and bar-tenders.

'I'll take the *Times*, Joey.'

'Hey, Dick. Where ya been? You look good, boy. Real good.'

I gave him a tip I couldn't spare. It was time to go and see Louise. I packed my bag and phoned Sherman House from the hotel. I had an image of Louise rolling up in one of the cars, collecting me and us racing back to... The operator told me that the number had been disconnected. I asked when and she said she couldn't give me that information.

'Why not?' I snarled.

'Do you wish to speak to the supervisor, sir?'

I was about to abuse her when I got a grip on myself. Disappointment was making me irrational. I paid my hotel bill and, with what was almost the last of my money, hired a car and drove out to Sherman Oaks.

Anyone brought up in the Australian bush, or maybe the country anywhere, will recognise the signs straight off — the grass growing high down the middle of the track, the earth surface unmarked except by wind and water, branches usually broken by passing vehicles mending themselves and starting to spring back. It had been some time since anyone had driven the last few hundred yards down the dirt road to Sherman House. The neglect became more obvious the further I went. There were weeds springing up on the tennis court and grappling with the flowers in the garden beds. I parked the rented Dodge near the swimming pool and could smell the rot and decay before I'd gone two steps. The pool was a green-grey, scummy mess. Leaves had fallen in and an animal — a squirrel or a rabbit, it was impossible to tell — had died there.

The horses had gone and the stable yard was dry and dusty, some of the dust being dried-out horse shit. A dripping tap had made a muddy runnel behind the stables, but otherwise nothing had happened there for a while. In a very short time the place had deteriorated to a point worse than it had been when Louise and I had taken it over and spent money on it. Being there wasn't much like coming home.

The house itself was empty with the power turned off, the windows closed and a musty smell in all the rooms. I had to force a side door to get in and I really need not have bothered. The telephone, of course, was disconnected. Everything of value — the carpets, the curtains, light fittings, the furniture, TV, record player, the refrigerator, golf clubs, rifles and tennis rackets — had been taken away. There were no clothes in Louise's closet and none in mine. There were no beds in the bedrooms, no desk or filing cabinets in the office. I sat on the stairs — from which the carpet runner had been removed — and felt like weeping.

Eventually I pulled myself together. I lit a cigar, a strange thing for an evidently bankrupt man to do, but it made me feel better. I remembered that one of our students, an aesthetic type who went by the name of Simon Verlaine, had had a drinking problem and was an expert at hiding bottles. His stint at Sherman House had been partly a drying-out exercise, not very successful. It had become a kind of game between us, hide and seek and the fifth, pint or hip flask. I went to the room he'd occupied and, sure enough, I found a half-full pint of Canadian rye whisky under a cut-out section of floor board. One of Simon's problems was that he tended to forget where he'd laid his plants. He's a big star now going by a different name after falling under the influence of a good woman, so I'd better not say any more about him.

I took a swig on the rye and decided to search the grounds on the off-chance I might find something useful or a clue as to what had happened. A few more swigs convinced me that things weren't too bad. Even if Sherman House was insolvent, the sale of the land and buildings would have to yield Louise and me *something*. The grass had grown and the leaves hadn't been swept up and shrubs and bushes knocked over by the valley winds hadn't been re-staked. The place looked as if it was rapidly headed back to the conditions it had been in when the Apaches had it.[56] The barbecue area which Rock and Liz had graced with their presences and where Jimmy Dean had drunk and arm-wrestled himself into a stupor, had become a rubbish dump where litter from the house and the cabins had been thrown. Stray dogs and other animals had rooted in the trash, spreading it over the whole area and flavouring it with their shit and piss. The depressing thought struck me that Sherman House wore an air of bad luck and was going to be trifle hard to sell. I had another drink to chase that thought away.

I wandered down a track past the cabin Charley Lucky had occupied and turned off near the creek to look at the smallest of the out-buildings — the one we usually allotted to the toughest of our clients. It had no electricity or hot water and the resident had to use kerosene lamps and a combustion stove. There was always some brave soul willing to take it, finding romance in chopping wood and trimming wicks. The cabin was surrounded by wistaria vine, passionfruit, and huckleberry bushes which had grown like crazy in the three months, practically concealing the place unless you knew where it was.

This cabin wasn't in good repair — there were possums in the roof and borers in the woodwork. I pushed aside the bushes to get a look at it, almost fearing that it might have fallen down, given the shape things were in. I was wearing my new sports clothes, not the outfit for this kind of work, and I swore when a bramble caught on my coat sleeve and my hat fell off as I ducked under a branch. I bent to retrieve the hat and felt something hard jab me in the kidneys.

'Stay right where you are. Stay bent over and don't look round.'

There was no mistaking that twang. Louise had acquired a Californian accent very quickly, essential for her TV work and even to be understood in LA. But the voice I heard then was the one that dated back to the hospital in Ceylon. Disobeying instructions, I straightened, turned and the hard object jabbed me again, more painfully.

'Louise, quit that! It's me, Dick!'

'Dick. Oh god, Dick. It can't be. It is! Oh, Dick, Dick.'

Very gratifying. She threw down the shotgun and launched herself at me, almost knocking me over. It was the first time I'd had my hands on a woman in three months — probably the longest dry spell in my life since I first wet my wick — and was bowled over by the feel and smell and taste of her. We embraced fiercely, kissing hard enough to rattle my newly-cleaned clackers and hugging like all-in wrestlers. We broke out of the clinch and she stepped back.

'Dick, you're so thin!'

And you're such a mess, was my thought. Fortunately I didn't say it, but it was true. Her hair was dull and grubby; without makeup, she looked younger but unkempt and the blue jeans, riding boots and dirty shirt made her look like a farm girl about to feed the hogs. This didn't blunt my enthusiasm for some more kissing and hugging but it did worry me. Louise saw the puzzlement on my face and kept herself beyond arm's reach.

'They took everything, Dick. Every bloody thing! I've been living here on what I could salvage, beg, borrow and steal. You seem to have been doing ok.'

There was a lot of accusation in that and with good reason from her point of view I suppose. Here I was in my smart clothes, toting a bottle of whisky and now brushing dirt from my hat.

'Jesus, Louise. I've been through hell.'

She picked up the shotgun. Not to use, I was sure, but the moment of unalloyed bliss was certainly over.

'Yeah, like what? I hear from you once in three fucking months and here you are, fit as a fucking fiddle, waltzing around in new clothes, half-pissed.'

'I...' Every instinct in me screamed to tell her, to give her all the details and wring from her every drop of sympathy. But I held back. Knowledge of what I'd been through and how it was orchestrated was dangerous. I was having trouble travelling with it myself, without loading it onto Louise. 'I can't tell you,' I said lamely. 'But it hasn't been pleasant.'

She sniffed and stuck out one rather dirty hand. Personal hygiene had always been one of Louise's obsessions, and I'd never heard her swear so much.

'Give me a drink,' she said.

We went into the cabin which Louise had managed to keep clean and tidy, mostly because there was so little in it. She was sleeping on a mattress, eating off a packing case, heating water on a paraffin stove, that kind of thing. We drank the rest of the whisky with slightly murky tap water and told our stories. Mine was heavily edited of course, but I conveyed the complete duplicity of the lawyer Brennan. I didn't say much about working on the movie and suggested that my subsequent disappearance had to do with the Luciano incident, although that was all cleared up now, I told her. I don't know how much she believed but I must have looked and acted sincere when I let her know that the grooming and new clothes were for her.

'If you think I'm thin now you should have seen me a week ago. I was like a scarecrow and dressed about the same.'

She nodded and kissed me, the first sign that fences were mending. 'You look good now. I like you thin.'

'I'm not planning to stay quite *this* thin.' I looked around the cabin. 'But there doesn't appear to be a lot to spare around here.'

'But you've got some money haven't you? You must have, to look like that.'

I opened my wallet and showed her the singles, the five, the ten. I had some change in my pockets and I produced that too.

'Jesus,' she said. 'We're really broke. Down and out in Hollywood.'

Her story was simple enough. The mob leaned on the bank and the bank foreclosed. The bank was a mob front and since we'd transferred all our accounts to it as part of the loan deal it was as easy as pie for them to take every cent. Sherman House was up for sale and our equity was nil. In fact if the sale price didn't reach our debt we were liable for the difference.

'That snake Brennan told me so,' Louise said. 'He added that he didn't think it likely to happen. The place is worth a lot to a developer. In a couple of years it'll be covered with houses.'

Brennan was obviously in with the mob *and* the FBI. Not so surprising now, after the Kennedy story and so on, but a bit of a facer back then.

'Didn't Bobby Silk recommend Brennan? I'll kill the little rat.'

'He did,' Louise said. 'Don't waste your time. I went to see him about it. All I can say is that he acted scared. Bobby's expanded — new office, branch in New York, more staff, new house and he's working on a new wife. Three guesses where the money's come from?'

It was brick walls every way I turned. Anywhere is a bad place to be without money, but Hollywood was one of the worst. Louise located some crackers and dry cheese and we sat down to eat like a couple of mice. She tried to get me to tell her more about what had happened but when she saw that I wouldn't open up she stopped.

I was beginning to wonder whether Simon Verlaine had left any other bottles about when Louise said, 'Television's booming. I'm sure I could get work again if I could present myself properly. But not like this.'

She was right. Under the grime and neglect she was probably better-looking than before, a bit more hollowed-out and dramatic-seeming. But while it was all right for Brando and Dean to turn up at parties in jeans and leather jackets, I hadn't heard that any women were doing it, and for that matter, as far as I know, they never have.

'We need a stake, Dick. Something to get us on our feet again. Think. There must be some way.'

'Does anyone owe you money? Were there any students who didn't pay their fees and have got work since?'

She shook her head. 'Wouldn't work. I had to sign away all rights to income like that or they would have thrown me in gaol. I really needed you then, Dick.'

'I'm sorry. I trusted Brennan and you said things were going all right.'

'Does anyone owe you money?'

Normally, I'd regard that as a ridiculous question. The boot was always on the other foot. But when I thought about it...

'Jimmy Dean,' I said. 'He owes me for four weeks' work in Texas.'

'How much?'

'A thousand bucks.'

Louise's smile almost lit up the gloomy space. We were in the room where she slept because the mattress was the only comfortable place to sit.

'He's rolling in dough,' she said. 'Just bought a new sports car for some fabulous amount. *Rebel without a Cause* is due out soon and they say he's terrific in it. You've got to go and see him, Dick.'

'Sure. Sure I will.'

She leaned back against the wall and started to unbutton her shirt. 'Not just now though,' she said. 'I wanna count your ribs.'

CHAPTER TWENTY-SEVEN

GETTING to see James Dean was no easy matter. He was working flat out on the *Giant* interiors and, given George Stevens' methods, that meant a lot of hours. He was also, apparently, doing a lot of partying, hanging out at the Villa Capri restaurant in Beverly Hills and hob-nobbing with the likes of Bogart and Sinatra. Word was getting around and Dean was hot, meaning that he was in demand and starting to be surrounded by the sort of protection that happens to a star in Hollywood. It's a matter of other people answering your phone, appointments to be kept or broken and games to play. I got him on the phone once at his Sherman Oaks house and he said to come on over. When I got there he was gone.

I hocked the shotgun Louise had managed to hang on to. It was a superb Purdey over and under we'd invested in when the money was flowing and it fetched enough to keep us in gasoline and basic groceries for ten days or so. The Dodge was overdue at the hiring agency but fortunately I hadn't given them the right address. 'Dick Kelly' had left Robert N. Silkstein's address, an inspiration I was now profoundly happy about. Still, come the end of the month when the rental companies took a serious look at what was outstanding, the hunt would be on.

Strangely enough, Louise and I were getting along famously through all this. Hiding out on the Sherman House grounds when at any time a buyer might turn up and the bulldozers might start rumbling, added a spice to our lives. Louise was the best of my wives, which is to say that she didn't nag very much. She understood that getting to see Jimmy Dean was difficult, especially after we'd spent a night together camped in our car outside his house to discover that this was one of the nights he'd spent elsewhere. He was running around with Ursula Andress at the time. We didn't know where she lived and had no way of finding out. It became a matter of hide and seek. I'd phone, get the run around, read the trades and try to anticipate where he might be. Bomb out and try again.

We cleaned out the swimming pool, pumped in some more water and kept ourselves fit swimming laps. We couldn't afford liquor or wine so drank a beer with lunch and another with our frugal dinner. We had coffee for breakfast. Lean and fit we were, but also broke, which counts for much more in Hollywood. For a time I worried about the FBI and the mob. Lucky might be safe in the arms of the Sicilian police, but did he still feel animosity about what had happened down in Tijuana?

Where was Johnny Stompanato, and was agent Burgess telling me all or any of the truth? These concerns I couldn't share with Louise and they made me edgy.

Eventually, with September running out fast, I heard that Dean had bought himself a new car, a Porsche Spyder, capable of more than a hundred miles an hour, and that he planned to race it at Salinas as soon as shooting on the movie finished. The only way to get to Salinas by road from Sherman Oaks was up Highway 41 and I was sure Dean would want to drive the new car. On 30 September, with fifty cents in my pocket and the certainty that the Ace car rental company would soon be sniffing for my spoor, I took up a position at the corner where even a lead-foot maniac driving from Sherman Oaks had to slow before joining 41.

I smoked my last cigar and waited. The Porsche came barrelling along, followed by another car, a station wagon, and I flagged it down. He'd have had to run me over not to stop.

'Hey, Jimmy.'

He took off his glasses and squinted. I was astonished at his appearance. Talk about aging, he seemed to have put on twenty years in the space of a couple of months. His hairline had been shaved and changed, his hair was grey and there were deep pouches under his eyes. This young man had been living and working hard.

'The fuck you doing?' he said.

'It's Dick Browning, Jimmy. Remember? I ran into a little trouble back there in Texas. With the cops, one thing and another. Maybe you heard.'

I never found out what story had been put about on my disappearance but it must have been good. Dean looked genuinely concerned as he stepped out of the car. I tried to look heroic. A youngish, dark-haired man was in the passenger seat. The station wagon pulled up behind and two men got out, lit cigarettes and waited.

'Hey, Dick,' Dean said. 'Yeah, man, that was a bad business. All that shooting. I'm glad to see you're ok. This here is Rolf Wuertherich, best goddamn mechanic in California. I'm off to drive in the races at Salinas. Why don't you come up?'

I shook my head. 'I've got some troubles, Jimmy, but it's nothing that the thousand bucks you owe me from Texas won't solve. Nice car.'

The Porsche was a silver grey, low-slung speed machine. It had the number 130 painted on it along with the words 'Little Bastard'.

'Ain't she a beauty? She'll do more'n a hundred and doesn't much like it under eighty.'

'Great,' I said. 'The movie all done?'

'Sure. Couple days ago.' He ran his hand over the dyed hair. 'I finished up aged around fifty somethin'. What d'you think about that?'

'I'm sure you did a great job. I need the money, Jimmy. I need it real bad.'

He took a packet from his pocket and flicked up one of his king-size Chesterfields. 'I can give you a check, Dick.'

'Where's the bank?'

'Beverly Hills.' He cackled in the way I'd heard so often. 'Hell, I got more money than you ever *dreamed* of havin'.'

I smiled. 'Make it out to cash.'

He lit the cigarette, ducking his head down to the flame from the lighter. He sucked in the smoke and let it filter out through his nose as he reached into the car and pulled out a jacket. He took a check book and a pen from a pocket, rested the book on the bonnet of the Porsche and scribbled. Then he tore the check out and handed it to me.

'Wish me luck, Dick.'

I examined the check — it was for a thousand dollars cash and he'd signed and dated it.

'Thanks, Jimmy.' I offered my hand and we shook. 'Good luck, you little bastard.'

He laughed, flicked his butt away and got into the car. He started the engine, gunned the motor and roared away onto Highway 41. The station wagon followed but I wasn't aware of it. I watched the grey Porsche until it was out of sight.[57]

NOTES

1 See *Browning Sahib* (1994).

2 Browning married Elizabeth Macknight, Coral Canetti (biga-
   mously and under a false name) and, after being divorced by
   Elizabeth Macknight, May Lin. See *'Box Office' Browning*,
   Browning in Buckskins and *Browning PI*.

3 Browning has already detailed two sojourns, approximately
   twenty years apart, in Canada in which he served, unwillingly,
   in the Royal Canadian Mounted Police and army, see *Browning
   Takes Off* and *Browning PI*. Given his career, this incident could
   have occurred at either time.

4 See *Browning Takes Off (1989)*.

5 Rocky Graziano (1922-90) was born Rocco Barbella in New
   York. He started fighting in the ring in 1942 after a violent
   and lawless adolescence. He held the world middleweight title
   briefly in 1947-8 after beating Tony Zale. He lost the title back
   to Zale in June 1948. Retiring from the ring soon after, he
   worked for some years in small acting roles on television and in
   films. His autobiography *Somebody up there likes me*, was filmed
   in 1955 with Paul Newman playing Graziano. The role was to
   have been played by James Dean.

6 Vicenzo De Mora, aka Machine Gun Jack McGurr, was a
   Chicago gangster. See *Browning Takes Off*, p. 142.

7 Nat Fleischer was for many years the editor of *Ring* maga-
   zine. The author of many books on boxing, he was the final

court of appeal in any dispute about the history and lore of pugilism.

8 'Slapsie' Maxie Rosenbloom held the world light heavyweight title in 1933-4. He was a clever boxer and light hitter, hence his nickname, who lost very few of his several hundred fights. He appeared in night clubs, on television and in films, often playing a punch drunk fighter. Max Baer won the world heavyweight championship in 1934 by beating Primo Carnera. He lost it the following year to Jim Braddock. His younger brother, Buddy, was a moderately successful heavyweight during and after the Second World War. Both appeared in films and on television, usually as 'heavies'.

9 Katharine Hepburn was an accomplished sportswoman who displayed her abilities most clearly in *Pat and Mike* (1952), in which she golfed with the legendary 'Babe' Didrikson and played tennis with the glamorous Gussy Moran. Browning was in Hollywood at the time and it was probably then that he helped her with her tennis.

10 Benjamin 'Bugsy' Siegel (1904-47) was a New York gangster, associate of 'Lucky' Luciano and Meyer Lansky, who is thought to have been an executioner in the east before he moved to the west coast to expand the activities of organised crime. He borrowed millions of syndicate dollars to build the unprofitable Flamingo hotel and casino in Las Vegas, eventually ran foul of powerful criminals and was shot to death in the Beverly Hills home of his mistress.

11 A German V1 rocket of a kind used against London in the blitz. Essentially, the V1 was a flying bomb with sophisticated navigational equipment installed.

12 Jack L. Warner and his brothers Harry, Albert and Sam — the principals of the Warners Bros studio.

13 Browning is mistaken. The Cheers' hit song 'Black Denim Trousers' which had the chorus:

He wore black denim trousers
And motor cycle boots
And a black leather jacket
With an eagle on the back
He had a hopped-up cycle {'sickle'}
That took off like a gun
That fool was the terror
Of Highway 101

was not released until 1956.

14 George Stevens (1904-75) was born into a theatrical family and was performing on the stage at a very early age. In Hollywood he moved from writing to directing shorts and eventually became a director of features. He was renowned for his painstaking craftsmanship, the amount of film he shot and the length of time he spent in the editing process. He won directing Oscars for *A Place in the Sun* and *Giant*. He directed successful comedies like *Woman of the Year* and *The Talk of the Town*, but perhaps his most enduring film was the western *Shane* (1953).

15 Hedda Hopper and Louella Parsons, famous Hollywood gossip columnists.

16 Charles 'Lucky' Luciano (1897-1962) was born Salvatore Luciana in Sicily and came to the United States at the age of ten. Growing up in the Lower East side of New York, he became a thief, narcotics trafficker and hit man. He participated in several gang wars in the 1920s and eventually came to control narcotics, vice and extortion rackets in New York. Arrested in 1936, he was tried and sentenced to fifty years imprisonment on a variety of extortion charges. He continued to direct criminal activities from gaol, and during the Second World War his influence was sought by authorities to stop a stevedoring strike that was hampering the war effort. His reward was a parole and deportation to Italy in 1946. In 1947 he travelled to Havana, Cuba for a top level meeting of American mafia

bosses, including Meyer Lansky and Frank Costello. American influence was brought to bear and he was deported from Cuba, returning to Italy after failing to gain admission to several Latin American countries. He is thought to have directed narcotics smuggling into the US from Europe until 1962 when he died of a heart attack in Naples. Through this period there were frequent unconfirmed rumours and reports of visits by Luciano to the United States.

17 See *Browning Takes Off*, pp. 136-43.

18 See *Browning PI*.

19 Vito Genovese (1897-1969) mafia chief, associate of Albert Anastasia in the notorious Murder Inc. organisation responsible for many gangland killings. Although instrumental, directly and indirectly, in many murders he was eventually convicted of smuggling and distributing narcotics in 1958 and was sentenced to fifteen years imprisonment. He continued to direct criminal activities and arrange the elimination of rivals such as Anastasia from gaol. He died of natural causes in Leavenworth penitentiary.

20 Browning had helped Federal agents frustrate the activities of a Hollywood chapter of the Ku Klux Klan in return for concessions about his status as an illegal immigrant. The FBI did not honour its undertakings to him, see *Browning in Buckskin*, pp. 162-87 and *Browning PI*, p.l.

21 In fact, Browning was nearing sixty, having been born in 1895, see *'Box Office' Browning*, p. 231. Throughout his memoirs he progressively reduces his age.

22 Al Hibbler was a popular singer of the 1950s who was blind. His version of 'Unchained Melody' was the number eight single on the *Cashbox* hits chart for 1955.

23 See *'Box Office' Browning*, pp. 8-9.

24 'Truck farming' was a system whereby vegetables were grown in rural areas and freighted to the cities in refrigerated rail and

road trucks. Previously, the vegetable needs of large centres were served by farms on their outskirts.

25 Roger Bannister, a twenty-five-year-old medical student, ran 3 minutes 59.4 seconds for a mile on 4 May 1954 at the university track in a match between the university and the Amateur Athletic Association. The first man to run the distance in under four minutes, he broke the previous record by almost two seconds.

26 On May 8, after a 55 day siege and battle, the French fortress at Dien Bien Phu fell to the forces commanded by General V. N. Giap. This marked the end of the French effort to retain its colonies in Indo-China.

'Crazy Man, Crazy' by Bill Haley and the Comets, released in April 1954, was the first 'mainstream' rock 'n' roll record. It did well but the follow-up record 'Rock around the Clock' attracted little attention until it became the theme song for the 1955 movie *Blackboard Jungle*. The song became the top *Cashbox* hit for that year. In 1954 Doris Day had a hit with 'Secret Love' and this may have been the song Browning heard.

27 In 1922 Browning was arrested in Canada for gun-running. In a manoeuvre that mis-fired, he took the place of a deserting member of the Royal Canadian Mounted Police and found himself serving in that corps in his stead. Browning eventually deserted himself. See *Browning Takes Off*, chaps 1-11.

28 The scene Browning refers to is a standard one in Westerns, but perhaps he had in mind the 1957 Gregory Peck movie *The Bravados* in which the action happens as he says.

29 The husband of Annie Oakley, brought to the screen by Howard Keel in the 1950 MGM musical *Annie Get Your Gun*.

30 See *Browning in Buckskin*, pp. 64-5.

31 Research into baseball, Olympic and boxing records has failed to reveal any trace of Slocum's alleged involvement. It is possible, of course, that, like Browning, Slocum was going under

another name in 1954. When Jack Dempsey knocked out the fifty-eight pounds heavier Jess Willard in Toledo, Ohio in 1919 in three rounds, it was widely rumoured that the tape around Dempsey's hands had been hardened by soaking in plaster of Paris. Jack Sharkey lost the world title to Primo Camera, who could neither box effectively nor hit hard. In 1933. Sharkey, accused of throwing the fight by almost everyone including his manager, maintained that Carnera had improved and that he was inhibited by the death of his friend Ernie Schaaf who had died after a fight with Carnera. See Peter Heller, *In this Corner: Forty World Champions tell their stories*, Simon and Schuster, New York, 1973, pp. 159-60.

32 The opening sequence describes the privately-owned airplanes converging on Jett Rink's birthday celebration as 'Monsters in a Jovian quadrille'. Edna Ferber, *Giant*, Gollancz, London, 1952, p. 5.

33 Dennis Hopper gives a slightly different version of this incident. In his introduction to *James Dean: Behind the Scene*, Leith Adams and Keith Burns (eds), Smyth Griphon, Los Angeles, 1990, p.9, he says that Dean told him why he had urinated as they were driving back to the hotel. He also says that there were about a thousand people watching. We know from other sources, e.g. John Parker, *Five for Hollywood*, p.104 that Dean was not living in a hotel but sharing a house with Hudson and Wills. Also it seems unlikely that Stevens, even if 'playing it smart' in the way Browning suggests, would have permitted a thousand people to watch the filming. Browning's account must be given equal credibility.

34 See Parker, *Five for Hollywood*, p. 104, for a reference to the death threats. According to this source, the antagonism was to sentiments expressed by both Bick Benedict and Jett Rink, as Browning surmised.

35 See *'Beverly Hills'* Browning.

36 In all probability this was Buddy Holly (1937-59) who had acquired a local reputation as a country singer before becoming a major recording star with his band, The Crickets. Along with two other popular singers, Holly died in a plane crash in January 1959.

37 See *'Beverly Hills' Browning, passim.*

38 In fact twenty-eight minutes.

39 See *'Box Office' Browning*, *'Beverly Hills' Browning'*, *Browning PI* and *Browning Battles On.*

40 *I've wined and dined on Mulligan stew*
    And never asked for turkey
    I've hitched and hiked and grifted too
    From Maine to Albuquerque
    Cole Porter, 'The lady is a tramp'

41 Department of Motor Vehicles.

42 Since 1966 American law officers have been obliged to inform arrestees of their right not to answer questions and to be represented by legal counsel. That year the Supreme Court reversed an Arizona court's conviction of Ernesto A. Miranda who had confessed to rape and kidnapping but had not been advised of his constitutional rights when arrested.

43 Clyde Barrow (1909-1934) was born in Telice, Texas and led a criminal life for almost all of his twenty-five years. Along with his brother Buck and Bonnie Parker, he went on a two-year spree of violent crime in the southwestern states — car theft, bank, store and gas station robbery, prison-breaking and murder. He and Bonnie Parker were shot to death by a posse in Louisiana in 1934. The pair died in what was literally a hail of bullets, 187 shots being fired.

44 Browning is referring to the 1967 Warner Brothers production of *Bonnie and Clyde*, directed by Arthur Penn who won the Academy Award for his effort. A highly romanticised but dramatically effective version of the Barrow/Parker story, the film

was critically and financially very successful and launched the career of Faye Dunaway.

45 See *'Box Office' Browning*, pp. 1-3; *'Beverly Hills' Browning*, pp. 176-9.

46 See *'Beverly Hills' Browning*, Introduction; *Browning in Buckskin*, *passim*.

47 John Edgar Hoover, Director of the Federal Bureau of Investigation under eight Presidents for almost 50 years, died in Washington, D.C., on 2 May 1972. This provides an approximate dating for the recording of this part of Browning's memoirs — to use his own expression, 'around 1982'.

48 See *Browning PI*, pp. 1, 206.

49 On 23 July 1934 a man, claimed by police and FBI to be the notorious bank-robber and prison escapee John Dillinger, was shot to death outside the Biograph theatre in Chicago by a police officer. Medical and other evidence supports the view that this man was a small-time hoodlum named James 'Jimmy' Lawrence who bore a physical resemblance to Dillinger, although having eyes of a different colour, a heavier build and lacking Dillinger's many scars. Some crime historians now believe that Lawrence's death was part of a carefully orchestrated plan, using criminals and corrupt police and officials, to provide Dillinger with a smoke screen behind which he disappeared forever. According to this theory, the FBI went along with the deception in order to gain kudos for its role in the supposed elimination of the then public enemy number one. See Jay Robert Nash, *Bloodletters and Badmen*, Evans, N.Y., 1973, pp. 176-8.

50 Browning was prescient. Lewis Hoad had not won a major singles title at this time, when American Tony Trabert was the world's leading player. In the following year Hoad would win three of the four 'grand slam' titles — the Australian, French and Wimbledon, and finish runner-up to Ken Rosewall in the American championship. Hoad possessed all the shots and

many authorities believe that, but for back injuries, he could have compiled an unrivalled record.

51 A species of small shark known as a 'gummy shark' was commonly eaten in many parts of Australia until the 1960s. Called 'flake' in some states, it is still the usual fish sold with chips and potato cakes in Melbourne fish and chip shops.

52 See *Browning in Buckskin*, pp. 82ff.

53 At the time Browning was writing, anti-biotics such as streptomycin had become available for the treatment of tuberculosis.

54 A further indication that Browning intended his memoirs to be published.

55 On September 21, 1955 Rocky Marciano, thirty-two-year-old world heavyweight champion, fought Archie Moore, then forty-one and the holder of the light heavyweight title. Marciano knocked Moore out in the ninth round. It was Marciano's last fight. He retired, undefeated as a professional, the only heavyweight title holder to do so.

56 As usual, Browning's grasp of anthropology was at fault. The Indians who occupied the area encompassing Sherman Oaks were members of one of the tribes collectively known as the Yuman.

57 James Dean was killed instantly on the afternoon of 30 September when his Porsche collided with a Ford sedan at the intersection of routes 466 and 42 at Cholmas, California.

www.ingramcontent.com/pod-product-compliance
Lightning Source LLC
Chambersburg PA
CBHW071511170626
46811CB00007B/2810

* 9 7 8 1 8 7 5 8 9 2 2 2 8 *